RAGGEDY ANN

一百周年纪念版

1918-2018

TO

MARCELLA

PREFACE AND DEDICATION

As I write this, I have before me on my desk, propped up against the telephone, an old rag doll. Dear old Raggedy Ann!

The same Raggedy Ann with which my mother played when a child.

There she sits, a trifle loppy and loose-jointed, looking me squarely in the face in a straightforward, honest manner, a twinkle where her shoe-button eyes reflect the electric light.

Evidently Raggedy has been to a "tea party" today, for her face is covered with chocolate.

She smiles happily and continuously.

True, she has been nibbled by mice, who have made nests out of the soft cotton with which she has been stuffed, but Raggedy smiled just as broadly when the mice nibbled at her, for her smile is painted on.

What adventures you must have had, Raggedy!

What joy and happiness you have brought into this world!

And no matter what treatment you have received, how patient you have been!

What lessons of kindness and fortitude you might teach could you but talk; you with your wisdom of fifty-nine years. No wonder Rag Dolls are the best beloved! You are so kindly, so patient, so lovable.

The more you become torn, tattered and loose-jointed, Rag Dolls, the more you are loved by children.

Who knows but that Fairyland is filled with old, lovable Rag Dolls—soft, loppy Rag Dolls who ride through all the wonders of Fairyland in the crook of dimpled arms, snuggling close to childish breasts within which beat hearts filled with eternal sunshine.

So, to the millions of children and grown-ups who have loved a Rag Doll, I dedicate these stories of Raggedy Ann.

Johnny Gruelle.

Holybird Children's Library

RAGGEDY ANN
STORIES
布娃娃安

（英汉双语版）

Written and Illustrated by
Johnny Gruelle

〔美〕约翰尼·格鲁尔 / 著　　向和平 / 译

天津出版传媒集团

天津人民出版社

图书在版编目（CIP）数据

布娃娃安：英汉对照 /（美）约翰尼·格鲁尔
(Johnny Gruelle) 著；向和平译. -- 天津：天津人民
出版社，2018.10
　（神鸟少儿馆）
　书名原文：Raggedy Ann Stories
　ISBN 978-7-201-14025-4

　Ⅰ．①布… Ⅱ．①约… ②向… Ⅲ．①儿童故事－美
国－现代－英、汉 Ⅳ．①I712.85

中国版本图书馆CIP数据核字(2018)第196865号

布娃娃安（英汉双语版）

RAGGEDY ANN STORIES

（美）约翰尼·格鲁尔 著　向和平 译

出　　版　天津人民出版社
出 版 人　黄　沛
地　　址　天津市和平区西康路35号康岳大厦
邮政编码　300051
邮购电话　（022）23332469
网　　址　http://www.tjrmcbs.com
电子信箱　tjrmcbs@126.com

责任编辑　伍绍东
封面设计　刘　亿
内文制作　刘增工作室（电话：13521101105）

制版印刷　三河市人民印务有限公司
经　　销　新华书店
开　　本　787×1092毫米　1/16
印　　张　7
插　　页　58插页
字　　数　180千字
版次印次　2018年10月第1版　2018年10月第1次印刷
定　　价　50.00元

CONTENTS

Raggedy Ann Stories
布娃娃 安

01

Introduction
布娃娃有了一个家

Before Reading

1. In this story, Marcella will find something special. Do you have something you found? What is it? Where did you find it?

2. Where is Marcella in the first picture? What can you see in the room?

3. What do you think Marcella will find in this room?

Marcella liked to visit her Grandma's old house. When she was at her Grandma's house, she played up in the attic. Marcella found many old toys and things there.

One day, Marcella was up in the attic as usual. She was tired because she was playing for a long time, so she sat down to rest.

She looked around and saw a box in the back of the room. "What could be in that box over there?" she thought. She stood up and climbed over some old chairs and tables. Finally, she got to the box.

玛塞拉喜欢去奶奶住的老房子里玩耍。在奶奶家，她时常爬到阁楼上，在那里发现了许多旧玩具和老古董。

一天，玛塞拉又像往常一样，来到阁楼上。她玩了很长时间，感到有点累了，便坐下来休息。

玛塞拉打量着四周，发现在房间深处放着一个盒子。她心中暗想："那个盒子里装着些什么东西呢？"想到这儿，她站起身来，翻过一些陈旧的桌椅，终于拿到了那个盒子。

She opened it, but it was too dark to see. Marcella brought the box over to the window where she could see better in the sunshine.

She found a little white hat and put it on her head. In an old bag, she found some dolls wearing old clothes. And there was a picture of a very pretty little girl with long hair. Then Marcella pulled out an old rag doll with only one button eye, a painted nose, and a smiling mouth. Her dress was made out of soft cloth. It was blue with pretty little flowers all over it.

Marcella was so happy. She picked up the rag doll and ran downstairs to show it to her Grandma.

"Well! Well! Where did you find her?" Grandma asked. "It's old Raggedy Ann!" Grandma gave the doll a hug. "I forgot about her. She has been in the attic for fifty years! Well! Well! Dear old Raggedy Ann! She needs her other eye right away!"

　　玛塞拉打开盒子，可是房间里光线太暗，她看不清楚。于是，她把盒子拿到窗户跟前，想借着阳光仔细地探寻一番。

　　首先映入玛塞拉眼帘的是一顶白色的小帽子，她顺手把帽子戴到了自己的头上。接着，在一个旧袋子里面，她找到一些穿着旧衣服的娃娃，还有一张留着长发的漂亮小姑娘的照片。最后，玛塞拉掏出一个破旧的布娃娃。这个娃娃的脸上只剩下一只纽扣眼睛，还有画出来的鼻子和一张笑嘻嘻的大嘴巴。布娃娃的裙子是用软布缝制的，蓝色的裙子上印着好看的小碎花。

　　玛塞拉高兴极了。她一把抱起布娃娃，三步并作两步地跑下楼去，拿给奶奶看。

　　"哎呦！天哪！你是在哪儿找到的？"奶奶问道。"这是布娃娃安！"奶奶拥抱了一下布娃娃。"我都把她给遗忘了。她在阁楼里已经待了整整五十年啦！哎呀！哎呀！亲爱的老布娃娃安！她急需得到另外一只眼睛！"

Marcella watched Grandma sew the button on Raggedy Ann. Grandma told Marcella how she played with Raggedy Ann when she was a little girl.

"Now," Grandma laughed, "Raggedy Ann, you have two new button eyes. Now you can see the changes in the world! And, Raggedy Ann, you have a new friend. I hope you and Marcella will have as much happiness together as you and I did!"

Then Grandma gave Raggedy Ann to Marcella. She said, "Marcella, this is my very good friend, Raggedy Ann. Raggedy, this is my granddaughter, Marcella!" And Grandma helped Raggedy Ann shake Marcella's hand.

"Oh, Grandma! Thank you so much!" Marcella said as she gave Grandma a hug and kiss. "Raggedy Ann and I will have so much fun."

And that was how Raggedy Ann became part of the doll family at Marcella's house. This book is about Raggedy Ann's stories.

玛塞拉看着奶奶给布娃娃安缝上纽扣眼睛。奶奶给她讲述了自己小时候与布娃娃安一起玩耍的故事。

"好了，"奶奶笑着说道，"布娃娃安，现在你有了两只新的纽扣眼睛，可以观看世上所发生的变化啦！布娃娃安，你又有了一个新朋友。我希望，你能够与玛塞拉共同度过一段幸福的时光，就像我们当年那样！"

说罢，奶奶将布娃娃安递给玛塞拉，郑重其事地介绍道："玛塞拉，这是我的好朋友布娃娃安。布娃娃，这是我的孙女玛塞拉！"奶奶帮助布娃娃同玛塞拉握了握手。

"啊，奶奶！太感谢您啦！"玛塞拉说着，张开双臂拥抱并亲吻了奶奶。"布娃娃一定会跟我玩得非常开心。"

就这样，布娃娃安变成了玛塞拉的娃娃之家中的一名成员。这本书所讲述的就是布娃娃安的奇特经历。

After Reading

1. Who is Raggedy Ann? What does Raggedy Ann look like?

2. What was Raggedy Ann missing?

3. You are a grandparent. You want to share something from your childhood with your grandchild. What would you give him or her?

Word List

 attic: *n.* a room in a house that is above all rooms and is right under the roof, often used as a place to keep things

 climb: *v.* to go up something high (such as a wall or a tree) by using one's hands and feet

 rag doll: *n.* a soft doll made from pieces of cloth

 button: *n.* a small, often round, piece of plastic on clothing, used to keep the clothing together

 hug: *n.* an action in which a person puts his/her arms around somebody else to show love

 sew: *v.* to repair clothes or attach something such as a button to them

Raggedy Ann Learns a Lesson
布娃娃安学到了一课

Before Reading

1. Raggedy Ann learns an important lesson in this story. What are three important lessons that children should learn?

2. Take a look at all of the pictures in this story. What do you think is going to happen?

3. Do you think the dolls will talk and do things on their own? Why do you think so?

Marcella's dolls were always very good and did not move while she was in the room. One day Marcella put her dolls against the wall. She told them to be good little children while she was away. When Marcella left the room, the Tin Soldier smiled at Raggedy Ann.

玛塞拉的娃娃们一贯表现出色，她每次来到玩具室，娃娃们总是待在原地一动不动。一天，玛塞拉把娃娃们靠墙摆好，叮嘱他们说，自己不在家的时候，他们一定要做个乖宝宝。玛塞拉刚一离开，白铁士兵就对着布娃娃安笑了起来。

When the dolls heard the front gate close, they knew that they were alone in the house. "Now let's have some fun," said the Tin Soldier. They all stood up. "Let's find something to eat."

"Yes, let's find something to eat," said all the other dolls.

"When Marcella took me to play outside today, we went to a door at the back of the house. I smelled something very good," said Raggedy Ann.

"Then you must take us there," said Lisa.

"I think it would be a good idea to make Raggedy Ann our leader for this trip," Uncle Clem said.

All the other dolls smiled and shouted, "Yes, Raggedy Ann is our leader!"

Raggedy Ann felt happy and said she would be their leader.

"Follow me," she said and started walking across the room.

The other dolls ran after her. They went through the house until they came to the kitchen door. "This is the door," said Raggedy Ann. Now all the other dolls could smell something good. They knew it would be very nice to eat.

听到前面大门关闭的声音，娃娃们知道家里的人出门去了。"现在让我们嬉戏玩耍吧！"白铁士兵说。于是，娃娃们全都站了起来。"我们还是先找点吃的东西吧。"

"对，我们先去找点吃的。"娃娃们齐声赞同道。

"今天，玛塞拉带我出去玩儿，我们经过房子后边一扇门的时候，我闻到了一股香味。"布娃娃安说。

"那么，你一定要带我们过去看看。"丽莎说。

"我认为，这次出行，让布娃娃安做我们的队长，应该是个不错的主意。"克莱姆叔叔提议道。

所有的娃娃都笑着嚷道："是的，让布娃娃安做我们的队长！"

布娃娃安感到很是开心，她表示自己愿意带队。

"跟我来，"说着，她迈步走向房门。

其他的娃娃赶紧跑步跟在她的身后。他们穿过房子，来到厨房门口。"就是这扇门，"布娃娃安说。这时，娃娃们全都闻到了一股诱人的香味。他们知道，厨房里的食物一定特别可口。

But none of the dolls were tall enough to open the door. They pulled. They pushed. But the door stayed closed. The dolls were talking and pulling and pushing.

At times one doll would fall down. Then other dolls would climb on her to open the door. But the door wouldn't open. Finally, Raggedy Ann sat down on the floor.

When the other dolls saw Raggedy Ann sitting with her hands on her head, they knew she was thinking.

"Shh, Shh!" they said to each other. They sat quietly in front of her.

"There must be a way to get in the kitchen," said Raggedy Ann.

"Raggedy says there must be a way to get inside," said all the dolls.

"I can't think clearly today," said Raggedy Ann. "It feels like I have a hole in my head."

Lisa ran to Raggedy Ann and took off her cap. "Yes, there is a hole in your head, Raggedy!" she said. Then she took a needle from her dress and used it to sew shut the hole in Raggedy's head. "It does not look very good, but I think I closed it!" she said.

但问题是，娃娃们的个头实在过于矮小，没有人能够摸着门锁。他们推呀，拉呀，可那扇门就是纹丝不动。

娃娃们议论纷纷，一个劲儿地推拉厨房的门。有时，一个娃娃会摔倒在地上，别的娃娃便踩着她去够门锁。但那扇门还是打不开。最后，布娃娃安在地板上坐了下来。

娃娃们看见布娃娃安用双手捂着脑袋，知道她正在动脑筋思考。

"嘘！嘘！"他们互相警示着，在她面前安静地坐了下来。

"一定有办法进入厨房，"布娃娃安说。

"布娃娃说了，一定有办法进去。"全体娃娃齐声重复道。

"今天我的头脑不太清醒，"布娃娃安说，"我感到头顶上好像有个洞。"

丽莎跑到布娃娃安的跟前，摘下她的帽子。"布娃娃，一点儿不错，你的头上真的有一个洞！"说着，她从裙子上取下一根针，开始缝补布娃娃头上的洞。"我缝的不怎么好看，但是我觉得还是把那个洞给补上了！"她说。

"I feel so much better!" said Raggedy Ann happily. "Now I can think clearly."

"Now Raggedy can think clearly!" shouted all the dolls.

"My thoughts were running out of the hole before!" said Raggedy Ann.

"They were running out, Raggedy!" shouted all the other dolls.

"Now that I can think clearly," said Raggedy Ann, "I think the door must be locked and to get in we must unlock it with the key. See, there is a key in the door!"

"But the lock is too high for us!" said Helen. "What can we do?"

"Yes, what can we do?" the Tin Soldier said.

No one had any idea.

After thinking for a minute more, Raggedy Ann said, "I know what we'll do." She asked Jumping Jack to try to open the door. Jack had a stick that was good for jumping. He jumped higher and higher on his stick. He jumped up to the key, turned it, and unlocked the door.

Then the dolls all pushed. The door opened.

The dolls ran into the kitchen. They all wanted to be the first to get to the food.

"我感觉好多啦！"布娃娃安快活地叫道，"这会儿，我可以清楚地思考了。"

"这会儿，布娃娃可以清楚地思考了！"娃娃们异口同声地嚷道。

"怪不得呢，我的好点子原来都从洞里漏掉了！"布娃娃安说。

"布娃娃的点子原来都漏掉了！"娃娃们齐声喊道。

"现在，我可以清楚地思考了。"布娃娃安说，"我想，门一定是锁上了，如果想要进去，我们必须用钥匙来打开锁。瞧，门锁上就插着一把钥匙！"

"只是锁太高了，我们够不着！"海伦说，"怎么办呢？"

"是啊，我们该怎么办呢？"白铁士兵接腔问道。

这下子，大伙儿都没有主意了。

布娃娃继续思考了一阵子，说："我知道该怎么办了。"她要求爱跳的杰克试着把门打开，因为他有一根助跳的棍子。靠着这根棍子，杰克越跳越高，终于一把抓住了钥匙。他使劲儿地转动钥匙，门锁咔嚓一声打开了。

娃娃们同心合力地一推，厨房门开了。

娃娃们争先恐后地冲进厨房，谁都想第一个拿到食物。

They quickly climbed up on the kitchen cupboard. They ran quickly and they pushed each other. One of the dolls pushed over a bottle of milk. The bottle fell on Lisa. The milk spilled out and made Lisa's dress wet.

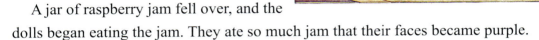

Uncle Clem found some bread. He sat down and started to eat it.

A jar of raspberry jam fell over, and the dolls began eating the jam. They ate so much jam that their faces became purple.

The Tin Soldier fell off the cupboard three times. But he climbed up again and again.

The dolls had so much fun. They ate as much as they could. Suddenly, they heard the front gate open.

They jumped to the floor and ran back to their room as fast as they could.

But they were too late. Just as Marcella came into the room, the dolls stopped moving.

"This is funny!" said Marcella. "They were all sitting in a line when I left! Why are they in different places now? Did my dog Fido move them?"

他们推推搡搡，飞快地爬上食品柜。有个娃娃不小心碰翻了一瓶牛奶。牛奶瓶砸到了丽莎的身上。牛奶流了出来，打湿了丽莎的裙子。

克莱姆叔叔发现一些面包。他马上坐下，大口吃了起来。

一罐树莓果酱歪倒在一边，果酱流了出来，娃娃们纷纷上前，没命地吞吃，以至于他们的脸都变成了紫红色。

白铁士兵从食品柜上一连掉下来三次，然而，他又一次次地爬了上去。

娃娃们吃得别提多开心了。他们一个个吃得肚皮滚瓜溜圆。突然，他们听到有人在打开前边的大门。

娃娃们迅速地跳起身来，朝着玩具室拼命地狂奔。

可是，他们迟了一步。就在玛塞拉走进房间的时候，娃娃们全都僵在了原地。

"真有意思！"玛塞拉叫道，"我走的时候，明明把他们摆成了一排。现在怎么散落了一地？难道是小狗菲逗干的坏事？"

Then she saw Raggedy Ann's face and picked her up. "Oh Raggedy Ann, you are covered with jam!" Marcella put Raggedy Ann's hand in her mouth. "Yes! It's jam! Oh, Raggedy Ann! You've been to the kitchen! The other dolls were with you, too!"

Then Marcella dropped Raggedy Ann on the floor and left the room.

When she came back, she picked up all the dolls and put them in a basket. Then she took them outside.

There, she washed all the dolls until they were clean. Then she hung them on the clothesline in the sunshine to dry. The dolls hung there all day.

就在这时，她看见了布娃娃安脏兮兮的小脸，伸手就把她拿了起来。"啊，布娃娃安，你怎么弄了一身果酱！"玛塞拉把布娃娃安的小手放进嘴里舔了一下。"是的！就是果酱！啊，布娃娃安，你跑到厨房去了！别的娃娃也跟着你一块儿去了！"

说罢，玛塞拉将布娃娃安丢在地上，转身离开了房间。

过了一会儿，玛塞拉回来了。她捡起所有的娃娃，把他们放进一个篮子里。然后，她把篮子提了出去。

玛塞拉打来清水，逐个地清洗娃娃们，将他们全都洗得干干净净。接着，她把娃娃们挂到晾衣绳上，放在阳光下晾晒。娃娃们在绳子上挂了整整一天。

"I think she washed my face so hard that my smile's almost gone!" said Raggedy Ann, after an hour of silence.

"No, it's still there," said the Tin Soldier.

Just then the wind blew strongly and Helen fell to the grass below.

Late in the afternoon Marcella came out with a table and chairs. Then she took all the dolls from the clothesline and sat them on chairs around the table.

They all drank lemonade and ate small cookies with sugar on them.

When they finished eating, the dolls were taken into the house. Marcella combed their hair and dressed them in pajamas.

Marcella placed them in their beds and kissed each one good night. Then she walked quietly out of the room.

The dolls did not talk for a few minutes. Then Raggedy Ann said, "I've been thinking!"

"Listen!" said all the other dolls, "Raggedy's been thinking."

布娃娃安在绳子上静静地待了一个小时之后，终于开口说道："我觉得，玛塞拉在给我洗脸时，用的劲儿太大，差点儿把我的笑容都给洗掉了！"

"没有洗掉，你的笑容依然很灿烂。"白铁士兵说。

就在这时，一阵强风刮了过来，把海伦吹落到了草地上。

傍晚时分，玛塞拉搬出来一张桌子和几把椅子。随后，她从晾衣绳上取下所有的娃娃，将他们摆放到桌子旁边。

大家开怀畅饮柠檬汽水，吃了很多甜蜜的小糕点。

吃饱喝足之后，玛塞拉把娃娃们搬进房间，给他们梳理好头发，换上睡衣。

玛塞拉把娃娃们放在各自的小床上，挨个亲吻了他们，跟他们道了晚安，便悄悄地走了出去。

娃娃们沉默了几分钟后，布娃娃安突然说道："今天我一直都在思考。"

"听着！"所有的娃娃齐声说道，"布娃娃一直都在思考。"

"Yes," said Raggedy Ann, "I've been thinking. Marcella gave us nice things to eat under the trees to teach us something. I think she wanted to teach us that we must never take without asking. So let's remember this. We'll try never to do anything that makes the people who love us unhappy."

"Yes, let us all remember," cried all the other dolls.

And Raggedy Ann, with a happy look in her button eyes, lay back in her little bed. Her cotton head was filled with thoughts of love and happiness.

"是的，"布娃娃安说，"我一直都在思考。在大树底下，玛塞拉请我们享用了很多美食，其实是想教我们一个功课。我猜，她是想教导我们，以后不经过许可，绝对不可以擅自拿取食物。所以，我们要把这个功课牢牢记地在心里，以后再也不做使爱我们的人不愉快的事情。"

"对，让我们大家都牢记在心！"娃娃们齐声喊道。

布娃娃安的纽扣眼睛里闪耀着快乐的光芒，她一头躺倒在自己的小床上，她的棉花脑袋里充满了爱和幸福的感觉。

After Reading

1. What did Raggedy Ann and her doll friends do?

2. What did Marcella do with the dolls?

3. What lesson did Raggedy Ann learn? Do you think it's a good lesson? Do you know someone who took something without asking? What happened?

Word List

 leader: *n.* a person who directs a group of people

 kitchen: *n.* the room in a house where food is made

 needle: *n.* a small thin tool for sewing

lock: *v.* to close a door with a key so others cannot open it

 key: *n.* a small object used to lock and unlock a door

 cupboard: *n.* a place to keep things, usually in the kitchen

 spill: *v.* when a liquid spills, it flows out of its container by accident

 raspberry jam: *n.* a sweet, thick, and sticky paste made from raspberries; a raspberry is a type of small red fruit

 basket: *n.* something we use to carry things, hold things, or for a small pet to sleep in; it is often woven

 clothesline: *n.* a piece of rope or string tied between two poles; wet clothes are hung on it to dry in the sun

 grass: *n.* short little green plants that cover the ground in fields and gardens

 lemonade: *n.* a drink made with lemon juice, water, and sugar

 comb: *v.* to use a hair tool to make one's hair smooth and straight

 pajamas: *n.* soft clothes that are worn to bed

 cotton: *n.* soft cloth made from a plant

03

Raggedy Ann and the Washing
布娃娃安沐浴记

Before Reading

1. Who does the work around your house (washing dishes, washing clothes, cleaning up, and so on)? Do you help around the house? What do you do?

2. What is something different about Raggedy Ann's face in the first picture?

3. In this story, Raggedy Ann was washed. Guess what happened to her during and after the wash.

Dinah was the housekeeper for Marcella's family.

One day, Marcella's Mamma looked out of the window and saw Mar-cella run up to Dinah and take something out of Dinah's hand.

"Oh, Dinah! I can't believe you did that!" Mamma heard Marcella say to Dinah.

Then Marcella sat on the ground and put her head in her arm. She started crying.

戴娜是玛塞拉家的管家。

一天，玛塞拉的妈妈朝窗外望去，只见玛塞拉迎着戴娜跑了过去，从她手里夺过来一样东西。

接着，妈妈听见玛塞拉朝戴娜嚷道："啊，戴娜！我简直无法相信，你居然做出这种事情！"

说着，玛塞拉一屁股坐在地上，把脸埋在手臂里，哭了起来。

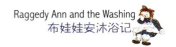

So Mamma went outside and sat down next to Marcella. "What's wrong, my love?" Mamma asked.

Marcella held up Raggedy Ann to show her mamma. Raggedy Ann looked so funny! Mamma had to smile when she looked at the doll.

Dinah could not understand why Marcella cried. She loved Marcella and did not want to make Marcella sad.

But Raggedy Ann was not sad at all. She knew that she looked funny, but she continued to smile. Her smile was wider than ever.

This is because Raggedy Ann knew what happened.

She remembered that morning when Marcella came to take off the pajamas from the dolls and dress them for the day. Marcella was already upset. She was not happy as she dressed each of the dolls.

Raggedy Ann thought at the time, "Perhaps she got up on the wrong side of the bed!"

And when it was Raggedy Ann's time to be dressed, Marcella was not careful. She was upset because she had hurt her finger when dressing Lisa.

Then Marcella heard her friend calling her name from outside. She threw Raggedy Ann on the floor and she ran quickly out of the room.

妈妈赶紧走出去，在玛塞拉的身边坐下，问道："宝贝儿，出什么事儿啦？"

玛塞拉举起布娃娃安，让妈妈看。布娃娃安的模样可真够滑稽的！妈妈看了之后，忍不住笑了起来。

戴娜不明白玛塞拉为什么哭泣。她喜爱玛塞拉，无论如何都不愿意惹她伤心。

布娃娃安却一点儿都不难过。她晓得自己的模样很搞笑，然而，她还是咧着嘴巴一个劲儿地笑，而且嘴巴咧得比平时更大。

因为布娃娃安知道所发生的一切。

她记得，那天早上玛塞拉过来给娃娃们脱去睡衣，换上白天的衣服。但不知怎么回事儿，玛塞拉的心情不太好。她在给娃娃们换衣服时，显得闷闷不乐。

布娃娃安在心里暗自嘀咕道："她也许是起错床了！"

轮到给布娃娃安换衣服了，玛塞拉有点儿心不在焉。她心里不太痛快，因为在给丽莎穿衣服时，她不小心弄痛了自己的手指头。

就在这个当儿，玛塞拉听见小朋友在外面喊她。她随手将布娃娃安往地上一扔，便快步跑了出去。

She didn't know that Raggedy had landed in the laundry basket.

A few minutes later, Dinah came into the room with some dirty clothes to be washed. She put them all on top of Raggedy Ann.

Then Dinah carried the basket out to the back of the house and washed them.

Dinah put all the clothes into a big pot and poured water on them.

Then she put the pot on the stove.

When the water began to get warm, Raggedy Ann climbed on top of the clothes and looked out of the pot. There was so much steam that she couldn't see anything. Dinah could not see Raggedy Ann, either.

Dinah used a big stick to move the clothes around in the big pot. The clothes and Raggedy Ann moved around while the water boiled.

Then Dinah took the clothes out of the big pot one at a time and washed them. She finally got to Raggedy Ann.

她万万没有想到，布娃娃安一头栽进了洗衣篮子。

几分钟后，戴娜拿着一些要洗的脏衣服走了进来。她把脏衣服丢到了布娃娃安的身上。

然后，戴娜提起洗衣篮子，来到房子后面，开始洗起衣服来了。

她把脏衣服全都倒进了一口大锅，往锅里添上水。

随即，她把锅放到了火炉上。

水慢慢地烧热了，布娃娃安爬到脏衣服上边，朝锅外张望。不料，锅里的水蒸气上腾，到处白蒙蒙一片，她什么都没有看见。戴娜也没有发现布娃娃安。

戴娜拿起一根大木棍，搅动着锅里的衣服。锅里的水在沸腾，布娃娃安随着衣服在水中不停地翻滚转动。

接着，戴娜将衣服一件件捞出来，用手搓洗。直到最后，她才把布娃娃安从沸水中打捞出来。

Of course Dinah did not know that Marcella had thrown Raggedy into the laundry basket by mistake. She thought Marcella really wanted Raggedy Ann to be washed. So she put soap on Raggedy and washed her on the washboard.

Two buttons from the back of Raggedy's dress and one of Raggedy Ann's button eyes fell off. After washing Raggedy and all the clothes, Dinah tried to dry Raggedy Ann.

It was just then that Marcella came back and saw Raggedy.

"Oh, Dinah! I can't believe you did that!" Marcella cried and quickly took the wet Raggedy Ann from Dinah's hand.

That was when Mamma heard Marcella and saw her cry. Mamma held Marcella's hand and talked to her softly. Soon, Marcella stopped crying.

Dinah told everyone that she didn't know that Raggedy was in the wash until she took Raggedy from the big pot. When Marcella heard that, she began crying again.

当然，戴娜不知道玛塞拉是无意中将布娃娃丢进了洗衣篮子。她还以为玛塞拉真的想要洗涤布娃娃安。于是，她在布娃娃身上抹上肥皂，用力地在搓衣板上揉搓起来。

结果，布娃娃安的一只纽扣眼睛和连衣裙上的两个扣子都被搓掉了。洗干净之后，戴娜打算把布娃娃安拿出去晾晒。

就在这个时候，玛塞拉回家看到了布娃娃。

"啊，戴娜！我简直无法相信，你居然做出这种事情！"玛塞拉叫着，一把从戴娜的手中夺过湿淋淋的布娃娃安。

这就是妈妈在故事开头所看到和听到的那一幕。弄明白了事情的原委，妈妈拉着玛塞拉的小手，轻声细语地安慰她。很快，玛塞拉就不哭了。

戴娜向她们解释，直到从锅里捞出安，她才知道布娃娃混在了脏衣服堆里。听到这儿，玛塞拉又哭了起来。

"It was all my fault, Mamma!" she cried. "I remember now. I threw Raggedy Ann as I ran out the door. She fell in the laundry basket! Oh! Oh!" and she hugged Raggedy Ann tight. Mamma was not angry with Marcella.

Mamma knew Marcella already felt very sorry. So Mamma just put her arms around Marcella and said, "But just look at Raggedy Ann. She doesn't seem to be unhappy!"

Marcella wiped her tears away and looked at Raggedy Ann. Raggedy was all wet, but she had a funny smile on her face. Marcella laughed. And Mamma and Dinah had to laugh, too, because Raggedy Ann's smile was bigger than it had been before.

"Let me hang Raggedy Ann on the line in the bright sunshine for half an hour," said Dinah, "and she'll be fine again!"

So Raggedy Ann was put on the clothesline, out in the bright sunshine. There, she enjoyed the breeze and listened to the birds in a nearby tree.

　　"妈妈，都怪我！"她抽噎着说，"这会儿我想起来了。就在我跑出去玩耍之前，我随手把安丢在了地上，她一定是掉进了洗衣篮子！啊！啊！"她一边哭，一边紧紧地搂着布娃娃安。

　　妈妈没有生气，她清楚玛塞拉已经十分懊悔。于是，妈妈伸开双臂，搂抱着玛塞拉说："你抬头看一眼布娃娃安。她看上去可是开心得很！"

　　玛塞拉擦干眼泪，看了看布娃娃安。布娃娃浑身湿淋淋的，但是，她的脸上却绽放出滑稽的微笑。玛塞拉看了，不由得破涕为笑。妈妈和戴娜也忍不住笑了起来。因为，布娃娃安的嘴巴咧得更大，比平时笑得更加开心。

　　"我这就把布娃娃安挂到绳子上，在阳光下晒上半个钟头，"戴娜说，"她就会恢复原样啦！"

　　就这样，布娃娃安被挂在了晾衣绳上。她沐浴着灿烂的阳光，享受着清爽的微风，聆听着小鸟在附近的树上歌唱。

Every once in a while, Dinah went out to turn and pat Raggedy. Finally, Raggedy became soft and dry.

Then Dinah took Raggedy Ann into the house. She showed Marcella and Mamma how clean and sweet she was.

Marcella took Raggedy Ann up to her room. She told all the dolls what had happened to Raggedy. She also said that she was very sorry about being upset in the morning when she dressed them. Of course the dolls couldn't say anything, so they only looked at Marcella with love in their eyes. Marcella sat in her little red chair and hugged Raggedy Ann tightly in her arms.

Raggedy Ann looked up at Marcella sweetly with her one button eye. On her face was the same old smile of happiness and love.

　　每隔一会儿，戴娜就出来拍打一下布娃娃，将她掉转一个方向。最后，布娃娃终于晾干了，变得像以前一样柔软。

　　戴娜把布娃娃安拿进房间，送给玛塞拉和妈妈观看。啊，布娃娃安洁净如新，简直可爱极了！

　　玛塞拉把布娃娃安抱进玩具室，给娃娃们讲述了安的遭遇，并且道歉说，早上自己在给他们穿衣服时，心绪不佳，现在感到非常抱歉。当然，娃娃们什么话都没有讲，他们只是深情地望着玛塞拉。玛塞拉坐在自己的红色小椅子上，把布娃娃安紧紧地抱在怀里。

　　布娃娃安用剩下的一只纽扣眼睛爱慕地看着玛塞拉。她的脸上绽放出爱和幸福的微笑，跟以往一模一样。

After Reading

1. Why was Raggedy Ann washed?

2. Did Raggedy Ann enjoy the washing? How do you know?

3. Do you think it was okay for Marcella to be mad at Dinah? Why do you think so?

Word List

housekeeper: *n.*   a person who does housework for pay

upset: *adj.*   unhappy, angry

to get up on the wrong side of the bed: *idiom*   an expression to explain why some mornings someone wakes up and is upset for no clear reason

hurt: *v.*   make something or someone feel pain

laundry basket: *n.*   a basket that holds clothes that are dirty and need to be washed

pot: *n.*   a container for cooking *(In the story, Dinah used a pot for washing clothes, but most people no longer wash their clothes this way.   Nowadays, most people use a washing machine or wash their clothes by hand.)

stove: *n.*   a thing in the kitchen that uses wood, coal, gas, or electricity to heat up food or water

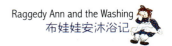

 steam: *n.* what water becomes when it is heated

 boil: *v.* to cook in water

 washboard: *n.* a board for washing clothes

 fault: *n.* something one did that caused an accident to happen

 tear: *n.* a drop of water that comes out of the eye when someone cries (the verb to tear has a different meaning)

 breeze: *n.* light, pleasant wind

 pat: *v.* to touch a person or animal quickly and gently with the flat of the hand to show kindness

04
Raggedy Ann and the Kite
布娃娃安和风筝

Before Reading

1. What activities do you enjoy doing outside with your friends?

2. In this story, Raggedy Ann flies high up in the air. What do you think might happen to her?

3. Look at the picture of Raggedy Ann and the birds. What do you think the birds are doing to Raggedy Ann?

One day Marcella was playing with her friends. Raggedy Ann was with her. The children were making a kite. They used sticks and cloth to make the kite.

They made a tail for the kite. Then they tied a large ball of string to the kite.

The kite was ready to fly now. One boy held the kite. A second boy held the string.

There was a nice wind, and the kite needed the wind to fly in the sky. The boy with the string said, "Let it go." The other boy held the kite up in the air. Then he let the kite go. The boy with the string started to run.

一天，玛塞拉同小伙伴们一起玩耍。她随身带着布娃娃安。孩子们正在扎风筝。他们用布和小棍儿来制作风筝。

他们给风筝安了个尾巴，最后把一大团线绳绑到了风筝上。

风筝制作完毕，孩子们准备放飞了。于是，一个男孩子手上拿着风筝，另一个男孩子紧紧地握着线团。

必须有风，风筝才能够飞上高天。恰好此时一阵风吹了过来。握着线团的孩子说："快放开风筝！"另一个孩子便将风筝高高举起，猛地松开了手。手握线团的孩子就跟着风筝跑了起来。

The kite flew very high in the sky. Raggedy Ann was happy to see it fly so high. But then something happened to the kite. It began flying this way and that way. The kite made four or five circles in the air. Then it fell to the ground.

"It needs a longer tail!" one boy said.

The children asked each other where they could get more cloth to make a longer tail for the kite.

"Let's tie Raggedy Ann to the tail," said Marcella. "I know she'll like to fly in the sky!"

The boys thought this was a good idea. So, they tied Raggedy Ann to the tail of the kite.

This time the kite flew straight up into the air. It flew very high. Raggedy Ann enjoyed being up in the sky. She could see very far. The children looked very small from the sky.

Suddenly, a strong wind came. She heard the wind singing as it pulled the kite faster and higher.

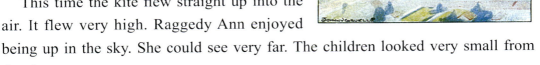

风筝升到了空中，高高地随风飞舞。看到风筝飞得这么高，布娃娃安非常高兴。但突然间，不知出了什么故障，风筝开始在空中左右摇摆。它一连转了四五个圈儿，便一头栽到了地上。

"风筝需要一条长点儿的尾巴！"一个男孩子说。

孩子们互相询问，不知到哪里再去找一些布条，好给风筝做一条更长的尾巴。

"我们把布娃娃安绑到风筝尾巴上吧，"玛塞拉说，"我知道她喜欢在天空飞翔！"

男孩子们觉得这个主意不错，他们就把布娃娃绑到了风筝尾巴上。

这一回，风筝"呼"的一声就飞到了空中，而且飞得很高。布娃娃安非常享受飞行的感觉，她能够看到很远的地方。她俯瞰地面，那些孩子看起来显得异常渺小。

忽然，一阵强风吹来，风儿裹挟着风筝越飞越快，越飞越高。布娃娃安听到了风儿的歌声。

Then, Raggedy Ann felt something tear. It was the cloth that tied her to the kite. As the wind blew harder, the tear became bigger.

Marcella saw Raggedy Ann fly high above the ground. She thought that Raggedy Ann was having a lot of fun. She also wanted to fly in the sky with Raggedy Ann.

After some time, Marcella grew tired of looking at the kite. She wanted to go home.

"Can you please pull down the kite now?" she asked the boy with the string. "I want Raggedy Ann."

"Let her fly some more," the boy said. "We'll bring her down later. We want to make the kite go higher!"

Marcella didn't want to leave Raggedy Ann with the boys, so she sat down to wait.

From the ground, Marcella couldn't see the wind tearing the cloth that held Raggedy Ann to the kite. Raggedy Ann could feel that she was not tied tightly any more. She was getting looser and looser.

Suddenly, the cloth tore all the way. Raggedy was not tied to the kite tail anymore! But she did not fall. The wind blew into Raggedy's skirt. She went flying away from the kite.

就在这一刻，布娃娃安感到有什么东西破裂了。原来将她绑到风筝上的那个布条裂了个口子。随着风力的加强，裂口变得越来越大。

玛塞拉看着布娃娃安在空中高高飞翔，知道布娃娃正在享受着极大的乐趣。她真心渴望自己也能够与布娃娃一道随风飘扬。

过了好一阵子，玛塞拉看风筝看得有点累了。她想要回家了。

"请你把风筝拉下来，好吗？"她向手握线绳的男孩子请求道，"我想取回布娃娃安。"

"让她再飞一会儿吧，"那个男孩子说，"很快，我们就会放她下来。我们想让风筝飞得更高一点儿！"

玛塞拉不愿意将布娃娃留在男孩儿们的手里，于是，她坐下来耐心等待。

在地面上，玛塞拉看不见风儿正在撕裂拴着布娃娃的布条。可是，布娃娃安可以感觉到布条越来越松，她越来越自由了。

就在这会儿，那个布条完全断裂了，布娃娃脱离开了风筝的尾巴！她并没有立即朝下坠落。风儿鼓起布娃娃的裙子，使之像伞一样大大地张开，朝着相反的方向飞去。

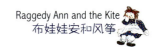

Marcella jumped up when she saw Raggedy Ann flying away from the kite. Without Raggedy Ann, the kite couldn't fly straight any longer. Finally, it fell to the ground.

"We'll get Raggedy Ann for you!" the boys said to Marcella. All the children ran to where the kite had fallen. They ran and ran. At last, they found the kite on the ground. But they could not find Raggedy Ann.

"Maybe she fell in your garden!" a boy said to Marcella. "The kite was above your garden when she fell!"

All the children went to Marcella's garden. But they did not find Raggedy Ann there.

Marcella was very sad. She went into her house and told Mamma what happened. Then Marcella went to her room and lay on her bed. Her Mamma went out to look for Raggedy Ann. But she couldn't find Raggedy Ann either. When Daddy came home in the evening he also looked for Raggedy Ann. But he could not find her. Marcella didn't want to do anything. She didn't want to play with any of her other dolls. And she cried for a long time that night.

看到布娃娃飘走了，玛塞拉"腾"的一声从地上跳了起来。这时，由于失去了布娃娃，风筝无法继续保持平衡，很快便一头栽到了地上。

"我们去把你的布娃娃拿来！"男孩儿们对玛塞拉说。他们撒开脚丫，朝风筝坠落的地方跑了过去。他们争先恐后地跑着，终于找回了地上的风筝。可是，布娃娃安却不见了踪影。

"也许她落到你们家花园里了！"一个男孩儿对玛塞拉说，"她坠落的时候，风筝正好在你们家花园的上空！"

孩子们又一窝蜂地跑到了玛塞拉家的花园里。不幸的是，他们在那里也没有找到布娃娃安。

玛塞拉无比伤心地回到家里，将所发生的事情告诉了妈妈。然后，她回到自己的房间，倒头睡在了床上。妈妈赶紧出门去寻找布娃娃安，结果却是扫兴而归。晚上，爸爸回家听说此事，也连忙出去寻找，仍然是一无所获。玛塞拉没有心情做任何事情，也不想跟其他的娃娃玩耍。那天晚上，她哭了很久很久。

Finally, she fell asleep. She dreamed that Raggedy Ann came back to her. She woke up crying. Mamma heard her and came to her bed. She told Marcella that in the morning Daddy would look for Raggedy Ann again.

"I shouldn't have given Raggedy Ann to the boys to tie to the kite!" Marcella cried, "I want her to come back to me."

Mamma took Marcella in her arms and said sweet things to her. But Mama thought that Raggedy Ann was lost and would never be found again.

Now, where do you think Raggedy Ann was?

When Raggedy Ann fell from the kite, the wind took her a long way. It took her to Marcella's garden. She fell into the top of a big tree in the garden. In the tree, two birds had a nest. They heard Raggedy Ann fall into the tree.

They were angry with Raggedy Ann for falling so close to their nest. Raggedy Ann did not move for a long time. The birds stopped being angry and became curious. They asked her who she was. But Raggedy Ann did not say anything to them. She did not move. She only smiled at them.

　　哭到最后，玛塞拉睡着了。她梦见布娃娃安又回到了自己的身边。玛塞拉哭着醒了过来。听见她的哭声，妈妈急忙来到她的床前，安慰她说，天亮之后，爸爸还会出门去寻找布娃娃安。

　　"我不该把布娃娃安交给男孩儿们，不该让他们把她绑在风筝上！"玛塞拉哭着说，"我想要她回家。"

　　妈妈将玛塞拉搂在怀里，对她说一些宽慰的话。但是，妈妈心里想的却是：布娃娃安丢了，再也找不回来啦！

　　那么，你认为布娃娃安会在哪里呢？

　　就在布娃娃安脱离开风筝的时候，风儿吹着她向前飘了好长一段距离，将她带到了玛塞拉家的花园里。她落到了园中的一棵大树上面。有两只鸟儿在那棵树上搭了个鸟窝。鸟儿们听到了布娃娃安坠落的声音

　　布娃娃安竟敢落到鸟巢附近，两只鸟儿气坏了。可是，布娃娃安躺在那里，好半天都没有动静。鸟儿们的愤怒逐渐变成了好奇。它们问道："你是谁呀？"可是，布娃娃安却一言不发，静静地躺在枝杈上，咧着嘴巴朝它们微笑。

Soon Mamma Bird told Daddy Bird, "See her hair! We can use it in our nest."

So the birds jumped closer to Raggedy Ann. They asked her if they could take some of her hair for their nest. Raggedy Ann did not say anything to them. She only smiled at them. So, the two birds pulled at Raggedy Ann's hair until they had some for their nest.

Evening came and the birds sang their lullabies. Raggedy Ann saw the stars come out in the sky.

The next morning, the birds pulled more hair from Raggedy Ann's head. They also moved her. Now, she could see the ground. She saw that she was in a tree in her own garden.

She saw Marcella looking for her again. Soon Marcella found Raggedy. And this is how she did it.

过了一会儿，鸟妈妈对鸟爸爸说："你瞧她的头发！我们可以用她的头发来垫鸟窝。"

于是，鸟儿们跳到了布娃娃安的身边，问道：我们可以取一些头发来垫鸟窝吗？布娃娃安依然默不作声，只是咧着大嘴巴一个劲儿地傻笑。两只鸟儿干脆用嘴巴来撕扯她的头发，拔出来一些铺在鸟窝里。

夜幕降临了，鸟儿们唱起了催眠曲。布娃娃安看见星星在天空上眨着眼睛。

第二天早上，鸟儿们又从布娃娃安的头上拔下一些头发，并且挪移了她的位置。这一下，布娃娃安可以看见地面了。她这才发现，原来她是在自家花园里的一棵树上。

她看见玛塞拉正在到处寻找她。很快，玛塞拉就找到了布娃娃安。事情的经过是这样的——

Mamma Bird had seen Marcella with Raggedy Ann in the garden many times. So she started singing, "Chirp! Chirp!"

Daddy Bird also started singing, "Chirp! Chirp! Chirp!"

Marcella looked up into the tree when she heard the birds singing. Then she saw Raggedy Ann in the tree.

She felt very happy. "Here is Raggedy Ann," she shouted.

Mamma and Daddy came out and saw Raggedy Ann. Daddy climbed up the tree and brought Raggedy Ann down. He put her in Marcella's arms.

"You'll never fly on a kite again, Raggedy Ann!" said Marcella, "I'll never let you leave me again."

So Raggedy Ann went into the house and had breakfast with Marcella. Mamma and Daddy were very happy when they saw Marcella playing with Raggedy Ann.

鸟妈妈曾经多次看见玛塞拉抱着布娃娃安在花园里玩儿。于是，它便扬声鸣叫起来："唧唧！喳喳！"

鸟爸爸也跟着放声高歌："啁啾！啁啾！啁啾！"

听见鸟儿的歌声，玛塞拉抬头朝树上望去，一眼便看见了树上的布娃娃安。

她喜出望外，大声嚷道："布娃娃安在这儿呢！"

爸爸妈妈赶了过来，看见了布娃娃安。爸爸立马爬到树上，把布娃娃安取下来，放进了玛塞拉的怀抱里。

"布娃娃安，你再也别想乘风筝飞行啦！"玛塞拉说，"我再也不允许你离开我了。"

玛塞拉抱着布娃娃安走进家门，一同吃了早饭。看到玛塞拉和布娃娃安在开心地玩耍，爸爸妈妈都高兴极了。

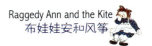

After Reading

1. What happened to Raggedy Ann after she was untied from the kite?

2. Who had the idea to put Raggedy Ann on the kite? Do you think it was a good idea?

3. Think of three things that are very special to you. What are some ways you can make sure you won't lose them?

Word List

kite: *n.* a toy made of paper and sticks that is made to fly in the sky with the help of a long piece of string

tail: *n.* a long thin rope tied to the back of the kite

string: *n.* a thin rope

tear: *v.* to break apart (usually cloth or paper)

nest: *n.* a bed that birds make with small sticks and anything soft; birds put their eggs in nests

curious: *adj.* interested in learning more

lullabies: *n.* gentle songs to put a baby to sleep

05

Raggedy Ann and the Painter
布娃娃安和油漆匠

Before Reading

1. Can you think of a time when a bad situation turned into a good one? What happened?

2. Look at the second picture. What is happening?

3. What do you think happens to Raggedy Ann in this story?

Marcella's Mamma wanted Marcella's room to be painted. The painters were coming early the next day. So, she put the dolls on a high shelf in the middle of the room.

The dolls had to sleep on the shelf that night. All the dolls lay on top of each other. Raggedy Ann had many dolls lying on top of her. She asked them to move. The dolls began moving to one side. Now Raggedy Ann was able to sit up.

妈妈想要粉刷玛塞拉的房间。次日一大早，油漆匠们就要过来。于是，玛塞拉将娃娃们放在了房间中央的一个高架子上面。

那天夜里，娃娃们只好在那个架子上过夜。他们互相叠压在一起，有许多娃娃摞在了布娃娃安的身上。布娃娃请求他们挪开一点。娃娃们努力往旁边挪了挪，布娃娃安这才坐起身来。

"Thank you, that is so much better," she said. "I'll be happy when morning comes!" she said. "Marcella will take us to the garden and play with us."

The dolls did not sleep that night. They sat and talked all night long. When it was morning, the painters came to work early. Marcella did not have time to move her dolls. She had to stay out of the way.

One of the painters was a young man. He saw the dolls and took Raggedy Ann down from the shelf.

"Look at this rag doll, Jim," he said to another painter. "She's nice." He began to whistle a song. He took Raggedy Ann by the hands and danced with her. She enjoyed the dance a lot.

The other dolls sat on the shelf and did not move. They did not want the men to know that the dolls were really alive. "Put her back on the shelf," said one of the other men. "The little girl will be angry with you."

But the young painter danced and danced with Raggedy Ann. Finally, he started throwing her up in the air and catching her.

　　"谢谢你们，我感觉好多啦！"她说，"等到早上，我们就舒服了。玛塞拉会带我们去花园里玩儿的。"

　　那个晚上，娃娃们彻夜未眠。他们挤坐在那里，整整聊了一夜。到了早晨，油漆匠们早早地就来了。玛塞拉根本没有时间把娃娃们搬出去，她只好独自待在外边。

　　有一位油漆匠是个年轻人。他看见娃娃们，便伸手从架子上拿起了布娃娃安。

　　"吉姆，你瞧这个布娃娃。"他对另一名油漆匠说，"她还蛮可爱的。"说着，他一边吹奏口哨，一边抓着布娃娃安的两只手，同她跳起舞来。布娃娃安很喜欢跳舞。

　　其他的娃娃们坐在架子上，连大气儿都不敢出。他们不愿意让人知道自己是有生命的。"快把娃娃放回到架子上，"一个油漆匠说道，"外面那个小姑娘会生气的。"

　　可是，年轻的油漆匠与布娃娃安跳个不停。最后，他开始将布娃娃安高高地抛在空中，再用手接着。

This was fun for Raggedy. As she flew up near the shelf the dolls smiled at her. They were happy for her.

But the next time the young painter threw Raggedy Ann up into the air, he couldn't catch her. Raggedy Ann fell into a bucket of paint.

"I told you!" said the older painter, "and now you will be in trouble."

"I didn't mean to!" said the young painter, "What should I do?"

"Put her back on the shelf!" answered the other man.

So the young painter put Raggedy Ann back upon the shelf. The paint on her head fell down onto her dress.

After breakfast, Marcella came into her room. She saw Raggedy with paint all over her and she began to cry.

The young painter felt sorry and told her what had happened.

"If you will let me," he said, "I'll take her home and clean her up. I'll bring her back in two days."

布娃娃安觉得这样非常有趣。她在架子周围起伏飞舞，娃娃们都面带微笑地望着她。他们为布娃娃安感到高兴。

年轻的油漆匠又一次将布娃娃安抛了起来，可惜这一回他没有能够接住她。布娃娃安一头掉进了涂料桶里。

"我跟你说过的！"年纪大的油漆匠呵斥道，"现在你遇到麻烦了吧。"

"我不是故意的！"年轻的油漆匠说，"我该怎么办呢？"

"把娃娃放回到架子上！"年长的油漆匠回答说。

于是，年轻人将布娃娃安放了回去。然而，涂料顺着布娃娃安的脑袋滴落到了她的裙子上。

吃完早餐，玛塞拉回到自己的房间。看到布娃娃安浑身沾满了涂料，她忍不住哭了起来。

年轻的油漆匠深感歉意，连忙向她解释，这是自己无意中犯下的过错。

"如果你同意的话，"他说，"我愿意把娃娃带回家去，将她清洗干净。过两天我再把她送回来。"

Marcella wanted Raggedy Ann to be clean so she agreed. That evening, the young painter covered Raggedy Ann in paper so he wouldn't get paint on himself, and he took her home.

All the dolls felt sad that night because Raggedy Ann was not with them.

"Poor Raggedy! I wanted to cry when I saw the paint all over her," said Lisa.

"She didn't look like our Raggedy Ann at all," said the Tin Soldier. He was crying.

"The paint covered her smile and nose. You couldn't even see her button eyes," said Helen.

And so the dolls talked that night and the next night. But in the daytime when the painters were there, the dolls stayed very quiet.

On the second day, the young painter brought Raggedy home. She looked clean, and Marcella hugged her and thanked the painter.

After dinner, Marcella came in and put Raggedy on the shelf with the other dolls.

When the house was quiet for the night, the dolls said, "Tell us what happened, Raggedy Ann!"

玛塞拉很希望布娃娃能够变干净，就答应了他的要求。当天晚上，年轻的油漆匠用纸将布娃娃安包好，以免涂料沾到自己身上。然后，他就把布娃娃带回家去了。

那天夜里，由于布娃娃安不在家，所有的娃娃都感到很郁闷。

"可怜的布娃娃！看见她满身都是涂料，我真想大哭一场。"丽莎说。

"她那副狼狈样儿，看上去完全不像我们的布娃娃安了！"白铁士兵说着，哭了起来。

"涂料遮住了她的鼻子和笑容，连她的纽扣眼睛也看不见了！"海伦说。

就这样，娃娃们谈论了一夜。第二天夜里也是如此。但是到了白天，当油漆匠们粉刷房间的时候，娃娃们全都默默地待在架子上。

两天后，年轻的油漆匠把布娃娃送回来了。布娃娃安看上去干干净净。玛塞拉把她抱在怀里，向油漆匠表示了谢意。

用完晚餐，玛塞拉走进房间，把布娃娃放回到架子上，让她和其他的娃娃们待在一起。

等到夜深人静了，娃娃们开口说道："布娃娃安，快给我们讲讲你这两天的遭遇！"

"Oh I'm so happy I fell in the paint!" said Raggedy. "I had the happiest time. The painter took me home. He told his Mamma why I was covered with paint. She took a rag and cleaned my button eyes. Then I saw that she was a very pretty lady."

"But the paint had gone inside my head," said Raggedy Ann. "It made the cotton inside wet. I couldn't think clearly. And my hair had paint in it."

"So the kind lady took off my hair. Then she opened my head and took out all the wet cotton. I felt so much better then."

"The next day, she washed the paint off of me. Then she hung me on the clothesline to dry. And while I hung out on the clothesline, what do you think happened?"

"We don't know!" all the dolls cried.

"Well, a little bird came and sat near me. She then picked cotton from my head to make her nest."

　　"啊，我真高兴自己掉进了涂料里！"布娃娃说，"我度过了一段非常美好的时光。油漆匠带我回家之后，向他妈妈解释了我沾满涂料的原因。于是，她拿来一块布，清理了我的眼睛。我这才看清楚，她是一位漂亮的女士。"

　　"但是，涂料渗进了我的脑袋，"布娃娃安继续讲道，"里面的棉花全都湿透了。我不能够清楚地思考。我的头发上也沾满了涂料。"

　　"那位好心的女士取下我的头发。接着，她拆开我的头颅，取出里面的湿棉花。我立刻就感到神清气爽。"

　　"第二天，她洗去我身上的涂料，把我挂在晾衣绳上晾干。就在我挂在晾衣绳上荡秋千的时候，你们猜，发生了什么事情？"

　　"我们猜不出来！"娃娃们异口同声地回答道。

　　"好吧，一只小鸟飞了过来，栖息在我的身边。它把我脑袋里面的棉花啄了出来，拿回去做窝。"

"Wasn't that sweet!" cried all the dolls.

"Yes, it was!" answered Raggedy Ann, "It made me very happy. When I was dry, the lady took me in the house again. Then she put new cotton inside me and sewed me up. She also put new hair on my head. Then she did something else, but it's a secret!" said Raggedy Ann.

"Oh tell us the secret!" said all the dolls.

"I know you won't tell anyone so I will tell you the secret. That is why my smile is bigger now," said Raggedy Ann.

The dolls all looked at Raggedy Ann's smile and saw that it was bigger than before.

"When the lady put the new white cotton in my body," said Raggedy Ann, "she also put a beautiful red candy heart inside me. So that is the secret. That is why I'm so happy! Feel here," said Raggedy Ann.

"太有意思啦！"娃娃们齐声嚷道。

"是啊，很有意义！"布娃娃安回应道，"这使我感到格外幸福。等到我晾干之后，那位女士把我拿进了屋子。她在我的身体里面放了新棉花，然后重新缝合起来。她还在我的头上安了新头发。后来，她还做了一件事，但那是一个秘密！"布娃娃安说。

"啊，快把秘密告诉我们！"娃娃们齐声恳求道。

"我知道你们不会告诉别人。我就把那个秘密告诉你们吧。这就是我的笑容为何更加灿烂的原因。"布娃娃安说。

娃娃们定睛端详着布娃娃安的笑脸，发现她的确比往日更加笑容可掬。

"就在那位女士将雪白的新棉花填充进我的身体时，"布娃娃安接着说，"她同时放了一颗漂亮的红色心形糖果在我的胸腔里面。这就是那个秘密，这就是我为什么这样开心的原因！你们来摸摸这里。"

All the dolls could feel Raggedy Ann's beautiful new heart and they were very happy for her.

After a while the Tin Soldier asked, "Is something written on your new heart Raggedy Ann?"

"I'm so happy you asked! I forgot to tell you," answered Raggedy Ann, "It says, 'I LOVE YOU!'"

娃娃们全都摸到了布娃娃安那颗美丽的新心，他们为她而感到满心欢喜。

过了片刻，白铁士兵问道："布娃娃安，你那颗新心上写了什么字吗？"

"你提出这个问题，太让我高兴啦！我忘记告诉你们了，"布娃娃安回答道，"那颗心上写的是'我爱你们！'"

After Reading

1. What happened to Raggedy Ann after she fell in the paint?

2. What is Raggedy Ann's secret?

3. Raggedy Ann's heart has a personal motto (a saying that helps remind her to do her best). What could be your personal motto?

Word List

shelf: *n.* a long flat board on a wall or in a cupboard used to put things on

whistle: *v.* to make a sound by blowing wind through the lips

to be in trouble: *idiom.* to make someone else angry about what you have done

06
Raggedy Ann Saved Fido
布娃娃安营救小狗菲逗

Before Reading

1. Fido is a dog. Do you have a dog or a cat? What happens to pets that are lost?

2. Look at the second picture. What are the dolls doing? Why do you think they are doing this?

3. This story is about how Raggedy Ann saved Fido. Guess why Fido needed Raggedy Ann to save him.

It was the middle of the night. The dolls were all asleep in their beds. Only Raggedy Ann was not sleeping.

Raggedy lay in her bed. Her eyes were looking up at the ceiling. She put her hand up on her head several times. She was thinking.

半夜时分，娃娃们都在床上睡得正香，只有布娃娃安尚未入眠。

布娃娃安躺在床上，两只眼睛望着天花板，好几次把手按在脑袋上。原来她是在思考问题。

After a long, long time, Raggedy Ann sat up and said, "I've thought it all out."

When the other dolls heard this, they all woke up. They sat up and said, "Listen! Raggedy has thought it all out!"

"Tell us about it, Raggedy," said the Tin Soldier. "We hope they were sweet thoughts."

"Not very sweet thoughts!" said Raggedy. And she dried a tear from her button eyes.

"We haven't seen Fido all day, have we?"

"Not since early this morning," Lisa said.

"I'm worried," said Raggedy, "and if my head didn't have all this new cotton, I'm sure it would ache because of the worry! When Marcella took me into the living room this afternoon, she was crying. I also heard her mamma say, 'We'll find him! He will come home soon!' I knew they were talking about Fido! He must be lost!"

The Tin Soldier jumped out of bed. He ran over to Fido's basket.

"He's not here," he said.

过了好长一段时间，布娃娃安"腾"的一下子坐了起来，叫道："我想明白啦！"

听见她的喊声，娃娃们全都惊醒了。他们一个接一个地坐了起来，嚷道："听着！布娃娃想明白啦！"

"布娃娃，请你讲给我们听听，"白铁士兵说，"但愿你所思所想的都是一些甜蜜的想法。"

"恐怕并没有那么甜蜜！"布娃娃说着，擦去她纽扣眼睛上的一滴泪水。

"我们一整天都没有看到菲逗了，对吧？"

"从早上开始，我们就没有看见它。"丽莎回答。

"我很担心。"布娃娃说，"我的脑袋里若不是塞满了新棉花，我相信自己一动脑筋，头就会痛的！今天下午，玛塞拉带我到起居室去，她一直在哭天抹泪。我听见她妈妈说：'我们肯定能够找到它！它很快就会回家的！'我晓得她们说的是菲逗。小狗一定是丢了！"

白铁士兵从床上一跃而起，跑到了小狗的筐子跟前。

"小狗果然不在里面。"白铁士兵说。

"When I was sitting in the window at about noon," Uncle Clem said, "I saw Fido and a yellow dog playing out on the lawn. Then they ran out through a hole in the fence!"

"That was Priscilla's dog! His name is Peterkins!" said Lisa.

"I know poor Marcella is very sad about Fido," said Helen, "I forgot all about it until now. I was in the dining room at dinnertime. Then I heard her daddy tell her to eat her dinner and he would go out and find Fido."

"I think it would be great if we could show our love for Marcella. We can try and find Fido!" Raggedy said.

"It's a great plan, Raggedy Ann!" said all the dolls. "Tell us how to start."

"Well, first, let's go out on the lawn and see if we can track the dogs!" said Raggedy.

"I can track them easily!" said Uncle Clem, "I'm good at tracking things!"

"Then let's go right away!" said Raggedy Ann, as she jumped down from the bed. The other dolls followed her.

"大约正午的时候，我坐在窗台上，"克莱姆叔叔说，"看见菲逗和一条黄狗在草坪上玩耍。后来，它们从篱笆上的一个洞里跑了出去！"

"那条狗是普里西拉家的，名叫彼得金斯！"丽莎说。

"我知道，可怜的玛塞拉因着菲逗而伤心不已，"海伦说，"我把这件事给忘了，这会儿才想起来。晚饭时我在餐厅，听到玛塞拉的爸爸劝她吃饭，还说他要出去寻找菲逗。"

"我想，如果我们能够趁机表示一下自己对玛塞拉的爱，那就太棒了。我们可以尝试着去找找菲逗！"布娃娃提议道。

"布娃娃安，这个主意不错！"全体娃娃一致赞同道，"快告诉我们该怎么去做。"

"好吧，第一步，我们先到外边的草坪上，看是否能找到狗狗们的踪迹！"布娃娃说。

"我不费吹灰之力，便可以找到它们的蛛丝马迹！"克莱姆叔叔说，"因为我特别擅长跟踪追击！"

"那么，我们立刻就出发吧！"布娃娃安说着，从床上跳了下来。其他的娃娃也都照样而行。

The window was open. The dolls helped each other to climb up to the window. Then they jumped onto the soft grass below. Of course because they were dolls, the fall did not hurt them at all.

At the hole in the fence, Uncle Clem saw the trail of the two dogs. The other dolls followed him until they came to Peterkins's doghouse.

Peterkins was too big to sleep in the house, so he had a nice dog-house outside under a tree.

Peterkins was surprised to see the little dolls coming up to his doghouse.

Peterkins could see that they were Marcella's dolls. "Come in," Peterkins said. So all the dolls went into Peterkins's doghouse. They sat down and Raggedy told him why they had come.

窗户敞开着。娃娃们互相帮扶着爬上窗子。接着,他们纵身跳到下面柔软的青草地上。当然,由于他们是娃娃,所以并没有摔痛。

在篱笆洞口,克莱姆叔叔发现了两条狗的踪迹。娃娃们紧紧地跟随着他,来到了彼得金斯的狗舍。

彼得金斯是一条大狗,睡在房子里边不方便,普里西拉的家人在户外的树下给它建了个很气派的狗舍。

看到一群娃娃前来拜访,彼得金斯不禁深感意外。

它认出来这些都是玛塞拉的娃娃,就说:"进来吧!"于是,娃娃们走进彼得金斯的狗舍,坐了下来。布娃娃安向彼得金斯说明了来访的理由。

"I'm worried, too!" said Peterkins, "But I couldn't tell Marcella where Fido was. She cannot understand dog language, you know! This is what happened. Fido and I were playing the greatest game in the park. Then a big man came. He had a stick with a funny thing on the end of it and he came running towards us. We barked at him. Then Fido thought the man was trying to play with us so Fido went up too close. Then a terrible thing happened. That bad man caught Fido with the stick and carried him to a car. He threw Fido in with a lot of other dogs!"

"The dog catcher!" cried Raggedy Ann.

"Yes!" said Peterkins. He dried his eyes with his paws. "It was the dog catcher! I followed his car. I saw him put all the dogs into a big pen, so that no dog could get out!"

"Then do you know the way there, Peterkins?" asked Raggedy Ann.

"Yes, I can find it easily," Peterkins said.

"Then show us the way!" Raggedy Ann said, "We must try to get Fido back."

　　"我也正在担心呢！"彼得金斯说，"可是，我无法将菲逗所在的地方告诉玛塞拉。要知道，她不懂狗的语言！事情的经过是这样的：我和菲逗正在公园里做游戏，突然来了一个身材高大的人。他手里拿着一根棍子，棍子头上装了个稀奇古怪的玩意儿。他朝我们跑了过来。我们对着他汪汪直叫。菲逗误以为这个人是在逗我们玩儿，便跑到了他的跟前。就在这时，一件可怕的事情发生了。那个坏人用棍子套住了菲逗，把它抱到一辆汽车旁边，然后将菲逗丢进了汽车。那辆汽车里还关着许多别的狗狗！"

　　"偷狗贼！"布娃娃安脱口而出。

　　"完全正确！"彼得金斯说着，用爪子擦了擦眼睛，"那是一个偷狗贼！我悄悄地尾随在他的汽车后面，看见他把所有的狗狗都关在了一个大围栏里，使它们无法逃脱！"

　　"彼得金斯，这就是说，你认得去那里的路？"布娃娃安问道。

　　"是啊，易如反掌。"彼得金斯答道。

　　"那么，你来给我们带路吧！"布娃娃安说，"我们一定要把菲逗救出来。"

So Peterkins led the way across streets. The dolls all ran along behind him. Once, a strange dog ran out at them, but Peterkins told him to mind his own business. The strange dog went back to his own doghouse.

At last, they came to the dog catcher's place. Some of the dogs in the pen were barking at the moon and others were crying loudly.

There was Fido. He was all covered with mud. He was so glad to see the dolls and Peterkins! All the other dogs came to the side of the pen and looked at the strange dolls.

"We will try and let you out," said Raggedy Ann.

When the dogs heard this, they barked happily.

Then Raggedy Ann, the other dolls, and Peterkins went to the gate.

The gate had a latch to keep it closed. Raggedy Ann knew that she needed to lift the latch to open the gate, but the latch was too high for her. So Peterkins held Raggedy Ann in his mouth and stood up on his back legs so that she could lift the latch.

就这样，彼得金斯在前边带路。它穿过街道，娃娃们一路小跑紧随其后。走到半路，一条陌生的狗冲着他们跑了过来，彼得金斯告诉它别多管闲事。于是，那条狗乖乖地回到自己的狗窝去了。

最后，他们来到了偷狗贼居住的地方。在那个围栏里，有些狗对着月亮狂吠不止，还有一些狗则在那里大声哀嚎。

果然，菲逗也在里边，它的身上沾满了泥巴。看到娃娃们和彼得金斯，它简直高兴得忘乎所以！所有的狗狗都跑到了围栏边，望着陌生的娃娃们。

"我们会尽量想办法，把你们给救出去！"布娃娃安说。

听到这话，狗狗们兴奋地汪汪直叫。

布娃娃安、彼得金斯和其他的娃娃们聚集在围栏门口。

门上的栓紧紧地扣着。布娃娃安知道，只有把栓拔起来，才能够打开大门。可是，门栓太高了，她够不着。彼得金斯把布娃娃安叼在嘴里，然后用两条后腿直立起来，这样她就能够着门栓了。

When the latch was lifted, the dogs pushed and jumped against the gate. They pushed so hard that the gate flew open. It knocked Peterkins and Raggedy Ann into the mud. When the dogs ran out of the pen, they jumped on top of one another and barked loudly. The dog catcher woke up. The dogs ran away down the street. Fido helped Raggedy Ann to her feet.

Fido, Peterkins, and all the dolls ran after the other dogs as quickly as they could. The dogs turned the corner just as the dog catcher came out. He was still in his pajamas.

He stopped in surprise when he saw the dolls in white pajamas running down the street. He had no idea what they could be.

When they got to Peterkins's house, the dolls thanked Peterkins for his help. Then the dolls and Fido ran home. They had to hurry because the sun was getting ready to come up.

布娃娃安伸手将门栓拔了起来。围栏里面的狗狗们使劲儿地冲撞大门。大门被撞开了，彼得金斯和布娃娃安一下子被撞到了泥巴地里。狗狗们从围栏里拼命地冲了出来，它们互相挤压，疯狂地吠叫着。喧闹声将偷狗贼惊醒了。于是，狗狗们顺着街道四散狂奔起来。

菲逗连忙将布娃娃安扶了起来。菲逗、彼得金斯和娃娃们忙跟在狗群的后面，拼命地奔跑。狗狗们刚转过街角，偷狗贼就穿着睡袍走了出来。

他看见身穿白色睡袍的娃娃们正在街道上狂奔，不禁惊讶地停下了脚步。他想不明白，那到底是一些什么动物。

大家回到彼得金斯的狗舍，向它表示感谢。紧接着，菲逗跟娃娃们一道跑回家去。因为太阳很快就要升起来了，他们必须抓紧时间赶路。

Raggedy Ann Stories
布娃娃 安

When they got to their own home, they found an old chair out in the yard. After a lot of work, they finally got it to the window. They climbed up on the chair and entered the room from the window.

Fido was very thankful to Raggedy Ann and the other dolls. Before he went to his basket, he gave them each a lick on the cheek.

The dolls ran quickly into bed. They were very sleepy. Raggedy Ann said, "If my legs and arms were not filled with nice clean cotton, I'm sure they would ache. Since they're filled with nice clean white cotton, they don't ache at all. I know Marcella will be so happy in the morning when she finds Fido in his own little basket, safe at home. I'm so happy that I feel like my body is filled with sunshine."

Since the dolls were now all asleep, Raggedy Ann lay down and smiled happily.

　　回到家，他们在院子里找到一把旧椅子。费了九牛二虎之力，他们才把椅子搬到了窗户底下。他们先爬上椅子，再爬上窗户，最后由窗户跳进了房间。

　　菲逗非常感激布娃娃安和其他的娃娃。在返回自己的筐子之前，它在每个娃娃的脸颊上都舔了一下。

　　娃娃们飞快地爬上床去，他们困得眼睛都快睁不开了。布娃娃安说："假如我的胳膊腿儿里填充的不是柔软干净的棉花，我肯定会感到疼痛难忍的。幸好，我的四肢里塞满了雪白的棉花，因此一点儿都不痛。我能够想象得到，早上当玛塞拉发现菲逗躺在它的筐子里，已经安全地回到家中，她一定会乐得心花怒放。想到这儿，我感到自己的身体里好像充满了阳光，我感到无比幸福。"

　　娃娃们的脑袋刚一挨着枕头，便立刻睡着了。布娃娃安躺在床上，快乐地微笑着。

After Reading

1. Who is Peterkins? Why did the dolls need to see him?

2. How did Raggedy Ann save Fido?

3. The dolls and Peterkins had to work together as a team. Can you describe a time when you worked in a team to get something difficult done?

Word List

 ache: *v.* hurt

 lawn: *n.* an area of grass in a yard or garden

 fence: *n.* a thin wall around a house or area; it is often made of wood or wire

 track: *v.* to follow an animal or a person by following the marks or signs that they leave behind

 trail: *n.* the marks or signs that an animal or a person leaves behind as they go by

 doghouse: *n.* a house for a dog

 bark: *n.* the woofing sound that a dog makes

 terrible: *adj.* very bad

 dog catcher: *n.* a person who catches dogs, usually with a special stick

 paw: *n.* an animal's foot

 pen: *n.* a small place to keep animals inside

 mind his own business: *idiom.* not pay attention to what others are doing

 mud: *n.* soft, wet, sticky dirt

 latch: *n.* a small object to keep a door, gate, or window closed

 lift: *v.* to pick up

 hurry: *v.* to go or do something quickly

 lick: *v.* to touch with the tongue (in America, people often think that it is good when a dog licks someone's face)

 cheek: *n.* each side of the face below the eye

Raggedy Ann Stories
布娃娃 安

Raggedy Ann's Trip on the River
布娃娃安河中历险

Before Reading

1. Have you ever taken a trip on a river or by sea? How did you travel? Where were you going? What did you do on the trip?

2. What usually happens when things are dropped in the water? What do you think will happen to Raggedy Ann if she falls into a river?

When Marcella had a tea party in the garden, all of the dolls were invited. Raggedy Ann, the Tin Soldier, Lisa, and all the others were there.

After a lovely tea party with cookies and milk, Marcella thought that the dolls were very sleepy. She wanted to put them to bed. She told Raggedy Ann to stay in the garden and watch things.

玛塞拉在花园里开了个茶点派对，邀请所有的娃娃前来参加。布娃娃安、白铁士兵、丽莎和其他的娃娃都来了。

他们喝牛奶，吃糕点，享受了一个美好的茶点聚会。玛塞拉觉得，娃娃们都有点困倦了，就送他们上床去休息。她吩咐布娃娃安留在花园里看守东西。

So Raggedy Ann waited for Marcella to return. Earlier, Marcella had thrown little pieces of cookies to the dolls, and these pieces were now on the ground. Now little ants had come to eat them. Raggedy Ann watched the ants. Then she heard a puppy behind her. It was Fido.

Fido ran to Raggedy Ann. He turned his head this way and that and looked at her. Then he put his front feet out and barked in Raggedy Ann's face. Raggedy Ann tried to look very serious, but she could not hide the big smile on her face.

"Raggedy Ann, do you want to play?" Fido barked. Then he jumped at Raggedy Ann and jumped back again.

The more Raggedy Ann smiled, the more Fido jumped. He then caught the end of her dress and pulled her around, tearing her dress.

This was great fun for a puppy dog like Fido, but Raggedy Ann did not enjoy it. She tried to pull away, but Fido thought Raggedy was playing.

He ran out the garden gate and down a path across the field. Sometimes, he stopped and shook Raggedy Ann very hard and her head hit the ground. Then he threw Raggedy Ann high in the air. She turned over two or three times before she hit the ground again.

于是，布娃娃安就在花园里等候玛塞拉回来。先前，当玛塞拉将小块糕点分给娃娃们时，有不少糕点碎片掉在了地上。这时，小蚂蚁们纷纷赶来享用。布娃娃安正在观察蚁群，忽然听到身后传来了小狗的叫声。原来那是菲逗。

菲逗跑到布娃娃安的身边，摇晃着脑袋，望着布娃娃。接着，它伸出两只前爪，冲着布娃娃安的脸汪汪直叫。布娃娃安竭力摆出一副严肃的模样，可是她无法掩饰自己脸上灿烂的笑容。

"布娃娃安，你想出去玩吗？"菲逗吠叫道。说着，它跳到布娃娃跟前，又跳了回去。

布娃娃安笑得越是开心，菲逗就跳得越发有劲儿。最后，它干脆咬住布娃娃的裙边，把她拖来拖去，并且撕咬她的裙子。

对于小狗菲逗来说，这样做非常有趣。但是，布娃娃安并不喜欢。她努力想要挣脱出来，而菲逗却以为布娃娃安是在跟它玩耍。

它拖着布娃娃跑出花园大门，穿过田野中的一条小路。小狗不时地停下脚步，用力地甩动布娃娃，把她的脑袋撞在地面上。接着，它又将布娃娃高高地抛起。布娃娃在空中旋转了两三圈，这才摔到地上。

By this time, Raggedy had lost a piece of her dress and some of her hair was coming loose.

As Fido came near a stream, another puppy dog came running across the small bridge to meet him. "What do you have there, Fido?" said the new puppy dog as he ran up to Raggedy Ann.

"This is Raggedy Ann," answered Fido. "We are playing. We're having a great time!"

Fido really thought that Raggedy enjoyed being thrown around and high up in the air. Of course she didn't. However, the game changed. When Raggedy Ann hit the ground, the new puppy dog caught her dress and ran with her across the bridge. Fido ran and barked behind him.

In the middle of the bridge, Fido caught up with the new puppy dog. Each dog tried hard to get Raggedy Ann. As they played with her, she fell over the side of the bridge into the water.

此时此刻，布娃娃安已经变得蓬头散发，她的裙子也被扯破了。

菲逗拖着布娃娃来到一条小河旁边。这时，另外一条小狗跑过小桥，迎了过来。"菲逗，你拖的是什么呀？"小狗跑到跟前，问道。

"这是布娃娃安，"菲逗回答说，"我们正在玩耍。玩得甭提多开心啦！"

菲逗真的以为布娃娃安喜欢被拖来拖去，喜欢被它高高地抛在空中。其实，布娃娃一点儿也不开心。不管怎样，游戏突然发生了变化。布娃娃安刚一落到地上，新来的小狗就一口咬住了她的裙子，拖着她跑上了小桥。菲逗赶紧在后边追赶，一个劲儿地汪汪直叫。

就在小桥中央，菲逗追上了新来的小狗。两只小狗你争我夺，互不相让。它们一不小心，布娃娃安从桥上摔了下去，掉进了小河。

The puppy dogs were surprised. And Fido was very sorry. He remembered how good Raggedy Ann had been to him. He remembered how she had saved him from the dog-catcher. The water carried Raggedy Ann away. All Fido could do was to run along the stream and bark.

Now, the good thing is, Raggedy Ann floated nicely. This is because she was filled with clean white cotton and the water didn't soak through very quickly.

After a while, the strange puppy and Fido got tired of running. The strange puppy went home across the field. He acted like nothing was wrong. Fido walked home very sorry. His little heart was broken. He knew that he had made Raggedy Ann drown.

　　两只小狗大吃一惊。菲逗想起布娃娃安总是友好地对待自己，还想起布娃娃安如何从偷狗贼手里将自己营救出来，不禁感到十分难过。河水载着布娃娃安向前流淌。而菲逗所能够做的，就是沿着河岸一边奔跑，一边吠叫。

　　幸运的是，布娃娃安在水面上漂浮了很长的时间。因为她的身体里填充的是雪白的干净棉花，所以河水无法很快地将棉花浸透。

　　过了一会儿，陌生的小狗和菲逗都跑累了。于是，新来的那条小狗穿过田野，回家去了。看它的样子，似乎一切都很正常。菲逗则沉痛地走回家去，它的心都要碎了。它知道，是自己害死了布娃娃安。

But Raggedy Ann didn't drown—not at all. In fact, she floated and the water carried her along very gently. It felt like Marcella was holding her. She even went to sleep.

Raggedy Ann slept peacefully as she moved along with the water. Then she came to a pool with a big stone. She woke up when the water pushed her against the stone.

Raggedy Ann tried to climb on the stone. By this time the water had completely soaked through her nice clean white cotton. She was so heavy that she could not climb. So she had to stay there, half in and half out of the water. She watched the ants and frogs. The ants and frogs watched her.

Marcella and Daddy were looking for her. They found pieces of her clothes and hair all along the path and across the field. They followed the stream until they found her.

When Daddy got Raggedy Ann from the water, Marcella hugged her so tightly that the water ran from Raggedy Ann and made Marcella all wet. Marcella didn't mind it at all. She was just so glad to find Raggedy Ann again.

其实，布娃娃安并没有葬身河底——她并没有被淹死。河水携带着布娃娃缓缓地流动，她感到自己就像是在玛塞拉的怀抱里。她醺然进入了梦乡。

布娃娃安顺水漂流，安静地睡着。到末了，她漂进了一个池塘。池塘里竖立着一块大石头。水流将布娃娃冲到了石头旁边，她这才惊醒过来。

布娃娃安拼命地想要爬到石头上。可是，这会儿河水已经完全浸透了她里边的棉花，她的身体无比沉重。她把吃奶的劲儿都用上了，还是爬不上去。万般无奈，布娃娃只好待在原处，一半身子浸泡在水里。她观察着蚂蚁和青蛙，蚂蚁和青蛙也好奇地望着她。

这时，玛塞拉和爸爸正在到处寻找布娃娃。他们在田野和小路上发现了她的衣服碎片和头发。他们顺着小河往前搜索，终于找到了布娃娃安。

爸爸将布娃娃从水里打捞上来。玛塞拉紧紧地搂着她，水从布娃娃的身上流淌下来，将玛塞拉的衣服都打湿了。可是玛塞拉却毫不在意。找回了布娃娃安，她简直感到欣喜若狂。

They hurried home. Mamma was baking a cake so it was very warm by the oven. Marcella took off all of Raggedy Ann's wet clothes and placed Raggedy on a little red chair. Then she brought all of the other dolls in and read a story to them while Raggedy Ann dried.

After about an hour, Raggedy Ann was completely dry. Mamma said the cake was done. She took a wonderful chocolate cake from the oven and gave Marcella a big piece. Marcella and the dolls had more tea with the cake.

That night when everybody in the house was asleep, Raggedy Ann sat up in bed and said to the dolls that were still awake, "I'm so happy that I don't want to sleep. I think the water soaked me so much that my candy heart must have melted and filled my whole body! I'm not angry with Fido at all!"

Happiness is very easy to catch when we love one another and are sweet inside and out. All the other dolls were happy, too.

他们匆匆赶回家去。妈妈正在烤制蛋糕，烘箱旁边异常暖和。玛塞拉给布娃娃安脱下湿衣服，让她坐在一张红色的小椅子上。就在布娃娃安慢慢烘干的时候，玛塞拉将所有的娃娃都抱了过来，给他们读一本故事书。

大约过了一个钟头，布娃娃安完全干透了。妈妈说，蛋糕也烤好了。说着，妈妈从烘箱里取出一个香喷喷的巧克力蛋糕，她给玛塞拉切下来一块。玛塞拉和娃娃们分享着蛋糕，还喝了好多茶水。

那天夜里，等家里的人都睡着了，布娃娃安从床上坐起来，对尚未入睡的娃娃们说："我太高兴了，不想睡觉。我猜，由于河水把我完全浸湿了，我的糖果心脏一定是融化掉了，所以我整个身心都感到甜蜜蜜的！我一点儿也不怨恨菲逗！"

幸福是具有感染力的。当我们彼此相爱的时候，我们整个身心都会感到甜蜜蜜的。听到布娃娃安的话，所有的娃娃也都感到非常幸福。

After Reading

1. Do you think Raggedy Ann had a good trip on the river? What makes you think so?

2. Did Raggedy Ann get angry with Fido? Why did she or why didn't she?

3. Describe a time when someone made a mistake and something bad happened, such as what Fido did in the story. What did you do in that situation? Did you get angry? What should happen to the person who caused the bad thing to happen?

Word List

 ant: *n.*   a very small bug

 puppy: *n.*   a young dog

 hide: *v.*   to make it so that no one can see (a person or thing)

 path: *n.*   an opening in a field or forest that is easy to follow

 stream: *n.*   a small river

 catch up with: *idiom.*   to run after someone and get right next to them (caught is the past tense of catch)

 float: *v.*   to not fall to the bottom of the water but stay on top Example: Boats float in the water.

 soak: *v.* to fill up and cover something completely with liquid; to make very wet

 [someone's] heart is broken: *idiom.* feel very sad

 drown: *v.* to fall to the bottom of the water and die

 gently: *adv.* carefully, softly

 oven: *n.* something used to bake food

 chocolate cake: *n.* a sweet food that is baked in an oven

 melt: *v.* (ice, chocolate, butter, etc.) to turn into liquid from heat
Example: the candy melted: the candy became liquid like water

08

Raggedy Ann and the New Dolls
布娃娃安和新娃娃

Before Reading

1. What happens when a new boy or girl comes to your school? Do you talk about them? Do you welcome them?

2. Look at the second picture and describe the new dolls.

3. Do you think the new dolls are happy to come and live with Raggedy Ann and her friends?

One day Raggedy Ann was lying on the floor just where Marcella had dropped her. Her rag arms and legs were in all directions going everywhere.

Her hair was messy, too. Some fell on her face, hiding one of her button eyes. She had a big smile on her face.

There were two new dolls in the room. But they were saying bad things about Raggedy Ann.

一天，玛塞拉不慎将布娃娃安掉到了地上。布娃娃安趴在那儿，摊开四肢，好像一个"大"字。

她的头发乱糟糟的，有些头发还披散到了脸上，遮住了她的一只纽扣眼睛。可是，她依旧咧着嘴巴笑嘻嘻的。

玩具室新来了两个娃娃。他们俩正在议论布娃娃安。

"What a sad-looking doll!"

"She has buttons for eyes!"

"And look at her hair! It is just made of yarn."

"Look at those shoes! They are so old."

Raggedy Ann did not show that she heard the new dolls. She just lay on the floor with a smile on her face.

Maybe Raggedy Ann thought that the new dolls were right. It hurt Raggedy Ann to hear such bad things about her. But she lay without moving.

Helen did not like the new dolls saying bad things about Raggedy Ann. She loved Raggedy Ann and her big smile. She rolled off her doll chair and said, "Oh no!" in her quiet voice.

Uncle Clem also did not like what the new dolls said about Raggedy Ann. He walked in front of the new dolls and looked at them. But he could not think of anything to say so he put his finger on his mustache.

Marcella's aunt had sent the two new dolls to her this morning.

Marcella named them Annabel-Lee and Thomas, after her aunt and uncle.

"这个娃娃简直是惨不忍睹！"

"她的眼睛居然是用纽扣做的！"

"瞧瞧她的头发！那就是一团乱毛线。"

"快看那双鞋子！实在是破旧不堪。"

布娃娃安仿佛没有听见新娃娃们的难听话。她依旧面带微笑地趴在地上。

也许，布娃娃安认为新娃娃说的没错。不过，听到他们的闲言碎语，布娃娃还是很受伤害的。然而，她趴在地上没有动弹。

海伦不满意新娃娃们对布娃娃安评头论足。她热爱布娃娃安和她那灿烂的微笑。于是，海伦从椅子上滑了下来，用她那安静的声音说道："啊，不对！"

克莱姆叔叔也不喜欢新娃娃们对布娃娃安的诋毁。他走到新娃娃面前，打量着他们。但是，他不知道该说些什么，只好用手指捻着自己的胡须。

原来今天早上，玛塞拉的姑姑给她送来了两个新娃娃。

为了表示对姑姑和姑父的尊敬，玛塞拉给两个娃娃分别起了姑姑和姑父的名字：安娜贝尔-李和托马斯。

Annabel-Lee and Thomas were beautiful dolls. They wore pretty clothes and had real hair. Annabel's hair was red and Thomas's hair was blonde.

Annabel was wearing a silk dress. She wore a hat with long silk ribbons. Thomas was dressed in a suit. Both he and Annabel wore nice black shoes.

They were sitting on two of the little red doll chairs where Marcella had put them. They could see the other dolls from the chairs.

When Uncle Clem walked in front of them and pulled his mustache, they looked at him and said, "He has holes in his knees!"

This was true. Uncle Clem was made of wool and the insects had eaten his knees and part of his clothes.

Uncle Clem was hurt when the new dolls said this about him. But he could not say anything.

He walked to Raggedy Ann and sat near her. He brushed her hair away from her button eyes.

安娜贝尔-李和托马斯是两个漂亮的娃娃。他们穿着美丽的衣衫,头上装着真正的头发。安娜贝尔的头发是红色的,托马斯则是一头金发。

安娜贝尔身穿一件丝绸长裙,帽子上装饰着长长的缎带。托马斯穿着套装。他们的脚上穿着崭新的黑皮鞋。

玛塞拉把他们放在了红色的小椅子上。坐在那里,他们可以看见其他的娃娃。

就在克莱姆叔叔走到他们面前,揪扯自己的胡子时,他们俩盯着他看了一会儿,说:"他的两个膝盖上有洞!"

的确,克莱姆叔叔是用毛线制作的,虫子咬破了他的衣服和膝盖。

听到两个新娃娃这样谈论自己,克莱姆叔叔很是痛苦。可是,他连一句话也说不出来。

他只好走到布娃娃安那里,在她的身边坐下,将遮住她眼睛的那绺头发撩开。

The Tin Soldier also went and sat next to Raggedy Ann. "They do not know you like we do," he said.

"We don't want to be her friends!" said Annabel-Lee.

"And the soldier, too," laughed Thomas.

"You should be ashamed of yourselves!" said Lisa to Annabel and Thomas. "We'll be sorry that you have come here if you say bad things about us and laugh at us. We're all happy here. We all like each other."

Marcella came in to get the dolls ready for bed and kiss them good night. She did not have pajamas for the two new dolls. So, that night she could not change them. She let them sit up in the two little red doll chairs so they would not make their clothes dirty. "I will make pajamas for you tomorrow," she said as she kissed them good night. Then she changed Raggedy Ann's clothes, put her in bed and gave her a good night kiss. "Take good care of all my children, Raggedy!" she said as she went out.

Annabel and Thomas talked quietly to each together. "I think we've been too quick to talk so badly about Raggedy Ann," said Annabel-Lee. "Marcella likes Raggedy Ann the most."

白铁士兵也走了过来，挨着布娃娃安坐下。"他们不像我们这样了解你。"他说。

"我们可不想跟她交朋友！"安娜贝尔－李说。

"也不想跟士兵做朋友。"托马斯笑着说道。

"你们应当感到羞愧！"丽莎对安娜贝尔和托马斯说道，"如果你们说别人的坏话，并且嘲笑别人，我们会感到难过的。因为以前我们在这里都很快乐，大家彼此悦纳。"

这时，玛塞拉走了进来。她送娃娃们上床睡觉，并且挨个亲吻他们，跟他们道一声晚安。她还没来得及为两个新娃娃预备睡袍，所以，这天晚上她无法给他们换衣服。为了不弄脏他们的衣服，她把新娃娃留在了红色的小椅子上。"明天我就给你们俩做睡袍。"说着，她亲吻了他们，说了一声"晚安"。最后，她给布娃娃安换好睡袍，把她放到小床上，吻了她一下。"布娃娃安，请你好好照看我所有的孩子们！"临走前玛塞拉说道。

安娜贝尔和托马斯悄悄地交谈起来。"我觉得，我们那样贬低布娃娃安，实在是太轻率了。"安娜贝尔－李说，"玛塞拉最喜欢的就是布娃娃安。"

"I'm sorry that we said bad things about her. Everyone is beautiful in different ways," said Thomas.

By now Annabel-Lee and Thomas were very tired after their long trip and soon they fell asleep and forgot about the other dolls.

When they were asleep, Raggedy Ann went quietly from her bed and woke up the Tin Soldier and Uncle Clem. The three of them went to the two beautiful new dolls. They picked them up and took them to Raggedy Ann's bed.

Raggedy Ann put them in her bed. She lay down upon the hard floor. The Tin Soldier and Uncle Clem tried to tell Raggedy Ann to take their bed. But Raggedy Ann would not do it. "I'm made out of soft cotton so I can sleep on the hard floor," said Raggedy Ann.

　　"我们说了她的坏话，我感到很抱歉。每个人都有自己独特的美。"托马斯说。
　　由于长途旅行，安娜贝尔－李和托马斯感到疲惫不堪。很快，他们俩就睡着了，将其他的娃娃们忘到了脑后。
　　看到他们酣然入睡，布娃娃安轻手轻脚地从床上爬了起来。她叫醒白铁士兵和克莱姆叔叔。他们一起走到两个漂亮的新娃娃跟前，齐心合力地抬起他们，把他们抬到了布娃娃安的小床上。
　　布娃娃安把床让给了他们，自己在坚硬的地板上躺了下来。白铁士兵和克莱姆叔叔都想把自己的床让给布娃娃，可是她却婉言谢绝了。"我是用柔软的棉花做的，所以我可以睡在坚硬的地板上。"布娃娃安说。

The next morning Annabel and Thomas woke up in Raggedy Ann's bed. They looked at each other and felt very ashamed because Raggedy Ann had given her bed to them.

They saw Raggedy Ann lying on the hard floor. "How good she looks!" said Annabel. "It must be her button eyes!"

"Her hair looks so beautiful!" said Thomas. "I didn't see how nice her face looked last night!"

"The others love her so much!" said Annabel. "It must be because she's so kind."

Both new dolls became silent. They were thinking.

"How do you feel?" Thomas finally asked.

"Very ashamed of myself!" answered Annabel. "And you. Thomas?"

"As soon as Raggedy Ann wakes up, I'll tell her I'm sorry," Thomas said.

"The more I look at her, the more I like her!" said Annabel.

"I'm going to kiss her," said Thomas.

"You'll wake her up," said Annabel.

But Thomas climbed out of bed and kissed Raggedy Ann on her cheek.

第二天早晨，安娜贝尔和托马斯一觉醒来，发现自己睡在了布娃娃安的床上。得知布娃娃安将自己的床让给了他们，两个新娃娃顿时面面相觑，深感羞愧。

他们看见布娃娃安睡在坚硬的地板上。"她看起来真美！"安娜贝尔说，"那一定是由于她的纽扣眼睛的原故！"

"她的头发也很靓丽！"托马斯赞叹道，"昨天夜里，我没有看清楚她那漂亮的脸庞！"

"大家都这么热爱她，"安娜贝尔说，"她一定非常善良。"

两个新娃娃沉默了，他们开始反省自己。

"你有什么感想？"托马斯终于开口问道。

"我感到羞愧难当！"安娜贝尔答道，"托马斯，你呢？"

"等布娃娃安睡醒了，我将立即向她道歉。"托马斯回答道。

"我越看布娃娃安，就越喜欢她！"安娜贝尔说。

"我想去亲吻她，"托马斯说。

"你会惊醒她的，"安娜贝尔劝阻道。

可是，托马斯已经从床上爬了下去，在布娃娃安的脸颊上亲了一下。

Annabel-Lee climbed out of bed, too, and kissed Raggedy Ann.

Then Thomas and Annabel-Lee picked up Raggedy Ann and put her in her bed. Raggedy Ann did not wake up. They went to sit in their two little red chairs.

After a while, Annabel said to Thomas, "I feel happier now."

"So do I!" Thomas replied.

Raggedy Ann lay quietly in bed where Thomas and Annabel had put her. She smiled. Her candy heart, which had "I LOVE YOU" written on it, was very happy to hear Annabel and Thomas.

As you know, Raggedy Ann had not been asleep at all!

安娜贝尔-李也从床上爬下来，亲吻了布娃娃安。

接着，托马斯和安娜贝尔抬起布娃娃安，把她放回到小床上。布娃娃安居然没有被他们惊醒。两个新娃娃又坐在了红色的小椅子上。

过了一会儿，安娜贝尔告诉托马斯说："现在我感到很幸福。"

"我也是！"托马斯说道。

布娃娃安静静地躺在床上。听到安娜贝尔和托马斯的话，她不禁莞尔一笑，她那颗写着"我爱你们"的糖果心脏简直乐开了花。

你要知道，布娃娃安其实并没有睡着！

Raggedy Ann Stories
布娃娃 安

After Reading

1. What did the new dolls think about Raggedy Ann and her friends?
2. How did Raggedy Ann become friends with the new dolls?
3. The new dolls talked about Raggedy Ann's clothes. Do you think a person's clothes can tell you about who they really are? Give some examples.

Word List

 mustache: *n.* hair above the lip on a man's face

 blonde: *adj.* hair that is yellow in color

 silk: *n.* an expensive type of cloth which is soft and shiny

 ribbon: *n.* a long piece of cloth or paper used to tie things or put in a person's hair

 suit: *n.* a set of clothes made from the same material, usually pants and a coat

 insects: *n.* a small creature that has six legs (examples: ant, bee, spider, fly)

 ashamed: *adj.* to feel bad because the person has done something wrong

09
Raggedy Ann and the Cats
布娃娃安和猫咪

Before Reading

1. Are dogs and cats usually friends? Do dogs and cats like you to play with their babies?

2. Look at the fourth picture. What do you think Fido and Raggedy Ann are doing?

3. Do you think Fido and the cat in this story will fight or will be friends?

Early one morning, Marcella came and dressed all the dolls. She put them all around her room.

She sat some of the dolls in the little red chairs around the doll table. There was a turkey, a fried egg, and an apple on the table. The food wasn't real. They were toys that were painted to look like real food. The little teapot and other doll dishes were empty, but Marcella told the dolls sitting at the table to enjoy their dinner while she was away.

一天清晨，玛塞拉进来给娃娃们换衣服。她把娃娃们摆成了一个圆圈。

她让一些娃娃坐在餐桌旁的红色小椅子上。桌子上摆着一只火鸡、一个煎鸡蛋和一个苹果。当然，这些食物都是假的，是一些足以乱真的玩具。桌上的小茶壶和小碟子全都空空如也。但是，玛塞拉却告诉娃娃们，她要走开一会儿，他们可以尽情地享用美食。

Lisa was given a seat on the doll sofa and Uncle Clem sat at the piano.

Marcella picked up Raggedy Ann. She carried Raggedy out of the room. She told the dolls, "Be real good children while Mamma is away!"

When the door closed, the Tin Soldier looked at Tom and gave the turkey to the penny dolls. "Would you like some nice turkey?" he asked.

"No thank you!" the penny dolls said in little penny-doll voices. "We've had all we can eat!"

"Should I play you some music?" Uncle Clem asked Lisa.

When they heard this, all the dolls laughed. They knew Uncle Clem could not play music. Raggedy Ann was the only doll who had ever taken music lessons. She could even play some songs with one hand.

In fact, Marcella almost wore out Raggedy Ann's right hand when she was teaching the song to her.

"Play something fun!" said Lisa. She covered her face with her hands and laughed. Uncle Clem began hitting the keys on the toy piano very hard. Then they heard a noise on the stairs.

丽莎被安排坐在了玩具沙发上，而克莱姆叔叔则坐在了钢琴前边。

玛塞拉抱起布娃娃安，就在临出门之前，她告诫娃娃们："妈妈不在家的时候，你们一定要做个乖宝宝！"

门关上了。白铁士兵看了看汤姆，把火鸡递给瓷娃娃们。"你们想来点美味火鸡吗？"他问道。

"不啦，谢谢你！"瓷娃娃们用细小的声音回答道，"我们已经吃饱了！"

"我能够为你弹奏一首乐曲吗？"克莱姆叔叔向丽莎问道。

听见这话，娃娃们全都哈哈大笑起来。因为他们清楚地知道，克莱姆叔叔根本不会弹琴。在他们中间，只有布娃娃安学过音乐，她甚至可以用一只手来弹奏歌曲。

实际上，在玛塞拉教布娃娃安练习弹奏的时候，布娃娃安的右手差点儿都要累断了！

"那么，你就弹奏一首有趣的曲子吧！"丽莎说着，用两只手捂着脸，笑了起来。克莱姆叔叔开始用力地敲击玩具钢琴的键盘。就在这时，他们听到楼梯上传来一阵响声。

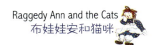

In the blink of an eye, all the dolls ran back to their places. They did not want real people to know what they were doing.

It was only Fido the dog. He put his nose in the door and looked around.

Fido could see the dolls sitting very still at the table. They were looking at the painted food. Uncle Clem was sitting still at the piano.

Then Fido pushed the door open and came into the room.

He walked over to the table and smelled the food. He hoped Marcella had given the dolls real food so that he could eat it.

"Where's Raggedy Ann?" Fido asked when he found out that there was no food.

"Marcella took Raggedy Ann and went somewhere!" all the dolls answered together.

"I've found something I must tell Raggedy Ann about!" said Fido, as he touched his ear.

转眼之间，娃娃们都跑回到自己的座位上。他们不愿意让人知道自己正在做些什么。

原来是小狗菲逗来了。它从门缝里探进脑袋，环顾着房间里的娃娃们。

菲逗看见娃娃们端坐在饭桌旁边，注视着桌上的食物。克莱姆叔叔静静地坐在钢琴前面。

于是，菲逗推开门，走了进来。

它径直走到饭桌前，嗅了嗅桌上的食物。它希望玛塞拉给娃娃们准备的是真正的饭菜，那样的话，自己就可以上饱餐一顿。

"布娃娃安在哪里？"菲逗没有发现可吃的东西，这才开口问道。

"玛塞拉带着布娃娃安出去了！"娃娃们齐声答道。

"我发现了一件事情，必须告诉布娃娃安！"菲逗抓挠了一下耳朵，说道。

"Is it a secret?" asked the penny dolls.

"Not at all," said Fido. "It's about kittens!"

"How lovely!" said all the dolls. "Real kittens?"

"Real kittens!" said Fido. "Three tiny little ones, out in the barn!"

"Oh, I wish Raggedy Ann was here!" said Lisa. "She'd know what to do about it!"

"That's why I wanted to see her," said Fido. "Let me tell you how I found them. This morning, I went into the barn to hunt for mice. Suddenly, Mamma Cat jumped at me very angrily. So I quickly ran away!"

"How did you know there were any kittens, then?" asked Uncle Clem.

"那是个秘密吗？"瓷娃娃们问道。

"也算不上是秘密，"菲逗说，"是关于小猫咪的。"

"太好啦！"娃娃们叫道，"是真的小猫咪吗？"

"是真的！"菲逗说，"有三只小猫咪，就在外面的库房里边！"

"啊，我真希望布娃娃安在这里，"丽莎说，"她肯定知道我们应该怎么办！"

"正是由于这个原因，我才过来找她。"菲逗说，"让我来告诉你们吧，我是如何发现小猫咪的。今天早上，我到库房里去逮老鼠。突然，猫妈妈愤怒地朝我扑了过来。我赶紧仓皇地逃跑了！"

"那你是如何知道库房里有小猫咪的呢？"克莱姆叔叔问道。

"I knew there must be something inside because she jumped at me that way! We are always very friendly, you know." Fido said. "I waited around the barn until Mamma Cat went up to the house. Then I went into the barn again. And I was so surprised! I found three tiny little kittens in an old basket. They were hidden in a dark corner!"

"Go get them, Fido, and bring them up so we can see them!" said the Tin Soldier.

"Not me!" said Fido. "If I had tin clothes like you have, I might do it, but you know, cats can scratch if they want to!"

"We will tell Raggedy when she comes in!" said Lisa, and then Fido went out to play with a neighbor dog.

Raggedy Ann came back to the room at bedtime. The dolls could hardly wait until Marcella put on their pajamas and left them for the night.

Then they told Raggedy Ann all about the kittens.

Raggedy Ann jumped from her bed and ran over to Fido's basket; he wasn't there.

"我心里清楚，猫妈妈如此凶狠地对待我，这里面一定有什么问题！你们知道，我和它以前一直非常友好。"菲逗说，"于是，我守候在库房周围，等到猫妈妈回房间了，我又再一次进入库房。我发现在一个阴暗的角落里，有三只小猫咪躺卧在一只旧筐子中！当时，我实在是大大地吃了一惊！"

"菲逗，快去把它们带来，让我们瞧一瞧！"白铁士兵说。

"我可不敢！"菲逗说，"假如我穿着你那样的白铁衣服，也许我还可以试一试。你们知道，猫儿急了会抓伤人的！"

"等布娃娃回来了，我们就告诉她！"丽莎说。于是，菲逗跑出去跟邻居家的狗玩耍去了。

到了晚上睡觉的时候，布娃娃安终于回来了。娃娃们急不可耐地想把这件事告诉她，可是，他们必须要等到玛塞拉给他们换好睡衣，吻别离开之后。

这时，他们才给布娃娃安讲了小猫咪的事情。

布娃娃安一下子从床上蹦了起来，跑到菲逗的狗窝跟前。可是，菲逗并不在里面。

Then Raggedy said that all the dolls could go out to the barn and see the kittens. They did this easily because the window was open and it was only a short jump to the ground.

They found Fido outside, near the barn. He was watching a hole.

"I was afraid something might hurt the kittens," he said. "Mamma Cat went away about an hour ago."

Raggedy Ann went in first. All the dolls followed her and went through the hole. Then they all ran to the basket.

布娃娃安说，那么我们就去库房看望小猫咪吧！娃娃们没有费多大的劲儿就跑了出去，因为窗子开着，他们只需要轻轻地一跳，就来到了外面。

娃娃们在库房附近发现了菲逗。它正全神贯注地盯着一个洞口。

"我担心有什么东西会伤害小猫咪，"它说，"大概一个钟头之前，猫妈妈出门去了。"

布娃娃安率先钻进洞里，其他的娃娃跟着她鱼贯而入。然后，他们朝那个筐子跑了过去。

Raggedy Ann started to pick up one of the kittens. At that moment there was a lot of noise, and Fido came running through the hole. Mamma Cat was behind him. When Mamma Cat caught up with Fido, he cried in pain.

Fido and Mamma Cat ran around the barn two or three times. Finally, Fido was able to find the hole and ran outside. Then Mamma Cat came over to the basket and saw all the dolls.

"I'm surprised, Mamma Cat!" said Raggedy Ann. "Fido has been watching your kittens for an hour while you were away. He wouldn't hurt them for anything!"

"I'm sorry," said Mamma Cat.

"You should trust Fido, Mamma Cat!" said Raggedy Ann. "He loves you."

"Thank you Fido!" said Mamma Cat.

"Have you told the people up at the house about your sweet little kittens?" Raggedy Ann asked.

布娃娃安伸手抱起一只小猫。就在这时，外面传来一阵喧闹声，菲逗从洞里窜了进来。猫妈妈紧紧地跟在它的后边。很快，猫妈妈追上了菲逗，把它抓得尖叫起来。

菲逗和猫妈妈绕着库房跑了两三圈。最后，菲逗找到了洞口，从那里逃了出去。猫妈妈这才来到筐子跟前，看到娃娃们。

"猫妈妈，我深感震惊，"布娃娃安说，"你不在家的时候，菲逗守护着你的小猫咪，它整整守了一个钟头。它绝对不会伤害小猫咪的！"

"我很抱歉，"猫妈妈说。

"猫妈妈，你应该相信菲逗。"布娃娃安说，"它爱你们。"

"谢谢你，菲逗！"猫妈妈去向菲逗表示了感谢。

"你有没有把可爱的小猫咪诞生的好消息告诉主人们？"布娃娃安问道。

"Oh, no, not at all!" cried Mamma Cat. "At the last place I lived, the people found out about my kittens. They took my kittens away. I never saw them again. I want to keep this a secret!"

"But all the people at this house are very kind. They would love your kittens!" said all the dolls.

"Let's take them right up to the room!" said Raggedy Ann. "Marcella can find them there in the morning!"

"What a great idea!" said all the dolls together. "Please, Mamma Cat! Raggedy Ann knows because she is full of nice clean white cotton and is very smart!"

So after talking with the dolls, Mamma Cat finally agreed. Raggedy Ann took two of the kittens and carried them to the house. Mamma Cat carried the other kitten.

Raggedy Ann wanted to give the kittens her bed, but Fido wanted to prove his love to the kittens. He kept asking Mamma Cat and the kittens to sleep in his nice soft basket. Finally, they did. So Raggedy Ann shared her bed with Fido.

"啊，没有，绝对不能告诉他们！"猫妈妈嚷道，"在我从前居住的那个地方，人们一发现我的小猫咪，立刻就会把它们送走。从此，我再也看不到它们了！我想保守这个秘密！"

"但是，这家的主人都很善良，他们会喜欢你的小宝贝的。"娃娃们齐声说道。

"让我们把小猫咪带到玩具室里，"布娃娃安说，"早上，玛塞拉就能够发现它们啦！"

"这个主意棒极了！"娃娃们异口同声地称赞道，"猫妈妈，请允许我们把小猫咪带走！布娃娃安知道该怎么做，因为她是用雪白柔软而干净的棉花填充的，她特别聪明！"

猫妈妈与娃娃们商谈了好久，最后总算答应了。布娃娃安抱起两只小猫咪，猫妈妈衔着另外一只，将它们带进了玩具室。

布娃娃安打算把自己的床让给小猫们，但是，菲逗想要表达它对小猫咪的关爱，一个劲儿地请求猫妈妈和小猫们睡在它那个舒适的筐子里。最后，它们接受了菲逗的好意。于是，布娃娃安邀请菲逗挤在她的床上休息。

The dolls could hardly sleep that night. They just wanted to see what Marcella would say when she found the little kittens in the morning.

Raggedy Ann did not sleep at all. Fido moved around too much and kept her awake.

In the morning, when Marcella came to the room, the first thing she saw was the three little kittens.

She cried out in excitement and carried them all down to show to Mamma and Daddy. Mamma Cat went along. She rubbed against all the chairs and doors. She was very proud.

Mamma and Daddy said the kittens could stay in the house and Marcella could have them all. So Marcella took them back to Fido's basket. Then she looked for names for them from a fairy tale book.

那天夜里，娃娃们几乎都难以入眠。他们迫不及待地想要知道，早上当玛塞拉发现小猫咪时，她会说些什么。

布娃娃安也是彻夜未眠。因为菲逗在那里不停地动来动去，害得她完全无法睡觉。

早晨到了，玛塞拉走进玩具室，一眼就看到了那三只小猫咪。

她兴奋地大叫着，把小猫们抱去给爸爸妈妈看。猫妈妈也跟着她前去，它摩擦着所有的椅子和门，感到无比自豪。

爸爸妈妈说，可以把小猫咪留在家里，归玛塞拉照看。于是，玛塞拉又把小猫咪送回到菲逗的筐子里。接着，她打开一本童话书，想为小猫咪选几个合适的名字。

Marcella finally decided on three names that came from storybooks: Prince Charming for the white kitty, Cinderella for the gray kitty and Princess Golden for the kitty with the yellow stripes.

So that is how the three little kittens came to live in the room with the dolls.

And it all turned out just as Raggedy Ann said earlier, because her head was filled with clean white cotton, and she could think really smart thoughts.

And Mamma Cat found out that Fido was a very good friend, too. She grew to trust him a lot more. She even let him help wash the kittens' faces.

后来，玛塞拉从故事书中选取了三个名字：白色的小猫叫魅力王子，灰色的小猫叫灰姑娘，黄色的狸猫叫金色公主。

就这样，三只小猫咪跟娃娃们住在了同一个房间里。

事情的发展正如布娃娃安所预料的。因为她的脑袋里装着雪白纯净的棉花，所以她能够想出绝妙的主意来。

猫妈妈发现，菲逗是一个非常可靠的朋友，所以越来越信任它，甚至让它帮着给小猫咪们洗脸。

After Reading

1. Why did Mama Cat hide her kittens?

2. What happened to the kittens in the end?

3. How do you know you can trust someone? What are things people do that show you can trust them?

Word List

 turkey: *n.*　a large bird that is cooked to eat

teapot: *n.*　a pot that heats and holds tea (a warm drink)

piano: *n.*　a musical instrument that has black and white keys and is played with the fingers

in the blink of an eye: *idiom.*　as fast as you open and shut your eyes; an expression meaning something is done very fast

barn: *n.*　a building outside of the house used to keep animals or farm tools

hidden: *adj.*　past participle of hide

scratch: *v.*　to use one's nails to rub or cut skin

trust: *v.*　to believe that someone is telling the truth; to believe that someone is not dangerous

rub: *v.*　to touch gently

stripe: *n.*　a line that goes up and down; a yellow striped (*adj.*) cat describes a cat with yellow lines and other color lines

10

Raggedy Ann and the Gift
布娃娃安和礼物

Before Reading

1. What would be the most wonderful gift in the world for your family?

2. Look at the third picture. What do you think Fido and Raggedy Ann are looking at?

3. What do you think is the gift in this story?

It was night time. The house was quiet. All the dolls were sleeping in their beds.

Fido was also sleeping in his basket. Every few minutes, he would wake up. He would open one eye and lift one ear. He knew something was going to happen.

Fido opened both his eyes. Then he smelled the air and got out of his basket. He shook himself and ran to Raggedy Ann's bed.

Fido put his cold nose on Raggedy Ann's neck. She raised her head from the little pillow.

夜晚，房子里静悄悄的。所有的娃娃都在床上做着美梦。

菲逗卧在自己的筐子里。每隔几分钟，它都要醒来一次。它往往会睁开一只眼睛，支楞起一只耳朵。因为，它预感到有什么事情就要发生了。

菲逗睁开双眼，在空气中嗅了一下，随即爬出了狗窝。它抖了抖身子，颠颠地跑到布娃娃安的床前。

菲逗将冷冰冰的鼻子伸到布娃娃安的脖子上。布娃娃打了个机灵，从小枕头上探起了脑袋。

"Oh! It's you, Fido!" said Raggedy Ann. "I dreamed the Tin Soldier put ice down my neck!"

"I can't sleep," Fido said to Raggedy Ann. "I feel that something is going to happen!"

"You have been eating too many bones, Fido. They keep you awake," Raggedy replied.

"No, it isn't that. I haven't had any bones since last Sunday. It isn't that. Listen, Raggedy!"

Raggedy Ann listened.

There was a sound like singing, from voices far away.

"What is it?" asked Fido.

"Shh!" said Raggedy Ann. "It's music."

It was the most beautiful music Raggedy Ann had ever heard.

It grew louder, but still came from far away.

Raggedy Ann and Fido could hear it well. It sounded like hundreds of tiny voices were singing together.

"啊！是你，菲逗！"布娃娃安惊叫道，"我梦见白铁士兵把冰块放到了我的脖子上！"

"我睡不着，"菲逗对布娃娃安说，"我感到有什么事情即将发生！"

"菲逗，你一定是吃了太多的骨头，撑得睡不着觉。"布娃娃说。

"不对，不是那么回事儿。从上个礼拜天起，我就没有啃过骨头。不是那么回事儿。布娃娃，你听！"

布娃娃安侧耳而听。

远处传来仿佛是唱歌的声音。

"那是什么声音啊？"菲逗问道。

"嘘！"布娃娃安说，"那是音乐的声音。"

那是布娃娃安所听到过的最美妙的天籁之音。

虽然还是十分遥远，但那个音乐声离他们似乎越来越近了。

布娃娃安和菲逗听得真真切切，好像是有几百个微小的声音在合唱。

Raggedy Ann Stories
布娃娃 安

"Please don't howl, Fido," said Raggedy Ann. She put her arms around the dog's mouth. Fido usually howled when he heard music.

But Fido did not howl this time. He felt happy listening to the song. He thought that something very nice was going to happen.

Raggedy Ann sat up in her bed. The room was full of a beautiful light. She thought that the music was coming from outside the window.

So she jumped out of her bed and ran to the window. Fido ran with her. They looked out of the window and into the garden.

　　"菲逗，请你千万别大声喊叫。"布娃娃安说着，伸出双臂搂住了菲逗的嘴巴。通常，一听到音乐声，菲逗就会汪汪大叫。

　　这一次，菲逗没有大声吠叫。美妙的歌声使它感到非常快活。它觉得，即将发生的一定是件好事。

　　布娃娃安从床上坐了起来。这时，玩具室里充满了迷人的霞光。布娃娃安觉得，那歌声是从窗外传进来的。

　　她从床上跳了下来，跑到窗户跟前。菲逗跟着她一块儿跑了过去。他们朝窗外张望，打量着花园深处。

Near the flowers, they saw many small fairies. Some were playing music and others were singing. Fido and Raggedy Ann listened to their song. The fairies started to dance closer and closer to Raggedy Ann and Fido. Raggedy knew that they shouldn't let the fairies see them. Fairies don't like to be watched.

Raggedy Ann said, "Hurry and go to your basket, Fido. They are coming here." Then Raggedy Ann ran back to her bed.

Fido jumped into his basket. He tried to look like he was sleeping. But he opened one eye to look at the fairies.

Raggedy jumped into her bed. She pulled the blankets up to her face. She also opened one eye to see the fairies.

Soon, little fairies came into the room through the window. They were shining like silver. And they were singing. They had a little bundle. A beautiful light came from this bundle. Raggedy Ann and Fido thought that it was like sunshine.

The fairies went across the room and out of the door with their bundle. Raggedy Ann and Fido heard them singing as they went down the hall.

　　就在花圃附近，他们看见了许多小仙女。仙女们有的在弹琴，有的在唱歌。菲逗和布娃娃安侧耳聆听着她们的歌声。仙女们开始翩翩起舞，离布娃娃安和菲逗越来越近。布娃娃心里明白，绝不能让仙女发现他们。因为仙女们不喜欢被人偷看。

　　布娃娃安说："菲逗，快回到你的筐里去。她们往这边来啦。"说着，布娃娃安跑回到自己的床前。

　　菲逗跳进筐里，竭力装出一副熟睡的模样。可是，它悄悄地睁开一只眼睛，看着外面的仙女们。

　　布娃娃安跳到床上，把毯子拉到脸上盖好。她也瞪大一只眼睛，从毯子缝里往外偷窥。

　　很快，小仙女们从窗户里飞了进来，像是银子一样闪闪发光。她们仍然在不停地唱着，有个仙女手里捧着一个小小的包裹，一道亮光从里面直射出来。布娃娃安和菲逗觉得，那道光芒很像是阳光。

　　仙女们带着那个包裹，穿过玩具室，走了出去。布娃娃安和菲逗听见她们在大厅里边走边唱。

Raggedy Ann Stories
布娃娃 安

After some time, the fairies came back. They did not have the bundle now. They all flew out of the window.

Raggedy Ann and Fido ran to the window again. They saw the fairies dancing around the flowers in the garden.

A little later the fairies' music stopped and they flew away. Then Raggedy Ann and Fido went back to Raggedy's bed to think about the fairies.

The next morning, the other dolls woke up. They saw Raggedy Ann and Fido looking curious and interested in something.

"What is it, Raggedy Ann?" asked the Tin Soldier and Uncle Clem.

Before Raggedy Ann could answer, Marcella came running into the room. She picked up all the dolls and ran down the hall. Fido ran with her, barking loudly.

过了不大一会儿工夫，仙女们回来了，她们捧着的那个包裹不见了。她们纷纷从窗户里飞了出去。

布娃娃安和菲逗再次跑到窗前，他们看见仙女们围着花园里的花儿载歌载舞。

不久，音乐声戛然而止，仙女们全都展开翅膀飞走了。布娃娃安和菲逗回到布娃娃的床上，思索着仙女们此行的目的。

到了早晨，别的娃娃醒了过来。他们发现，布娃娃安和菲逗的脸上带着好奇的神情，正在兴致勃勃地讨论着什么。

"布娃娃安，你们在聊什么事儿啊？"白铁士兵和克莱姆叔叔问道。

布娃娃安还没来得及回答，玛塞拉猛地冲了进来。她一把抱起所有的娃娃，跑进了大厅。菲逗跟在她的身后，大声地吠叫着。

"Be quiet!" Marcella said to Fido. "It's sleeping. You will wake it!" She took them to Mamma's bed-room. Mamma was in bed. Next to her was a smaller bed.

Mamma helped Marcella put the dolls in a circle around the small bed. The dolls could now see that a bundle was in the bed.

Mamma pulled back the blanket from the bundle. The dolls saw a tiny little hand, a little face with a small nose, and a little head with no hair. It was a baby boy!

Then Marcella took the dolls back to their room. They all started to talk at once.

"A little baby brother for Marcella!" said Uncle Clem.

"A beautiful bundle of love and fairy sunshine for everybody in the house!" said Raggedy Ann. Then she sat at the piano and played a happy song.

　　"安静！"玛塞拉命令菲逗说，"他正在睡觉，你会吵醒他的！"她把大家带到了妈妈的卧室。妈妈躺在大床上，旁边放着一张婴儿床。

　　妈妈帮助玛塞拉将娃娃们摆放在婴儿床的四周。这时，娃娃们才发现小床上放着一个包裹。

　　妈妈拉开包裹上的毯子。娃娃们看见一只小手和一个长着小鼻子的小脸蛋，以及光秃秃的小脑袋。原来那是一个男婴！

　　随后，玛塞拉把娃娃们送回他们的房间。顿时，娃娃们七嘴八舌地议论起来。

　　"玛塞拉添了个小弟弟！"克莱姆叔叔说。

　　"这是一个美好的爱的礼物，是仙女们送给家中每一个人的阳光！"布娃娃安说。她在钢琴前坐了下来，弹奏起一首欢快的歌曲。

After Reading

1. What did Raggedy Ann and Fido see that night?
2. Who was the baby?
3. What special things do people do when a baby is born?

Word List

pillow: *n.*   something you put your head on in bed

howl: *v.*   to make a loud and long cry (a dog)

fairy: *n.*   a very small magical person

blanket: *n.*   cloth on the bed to keep you warm when you sleep

silver: *adj.*   shiny, grayish color

bundle: *n.*   a small package

hall: *n.*   the space you can walk between rooms

11

Raggedy Ann and the Chickens
布娃娃安和鸡宝宝

Before Reading

1. What does a mother chicken do to help her eggs become chickens?

2. In this story, Raggedy Ann fell into the place where the chickens lived. What do you think will happen to her?

3. Look at the last picture. What is Raggedy Ann doing? Why do you think she is doing it?

When Marcella had to run into the house, she left Raggedy sitting on the fence by the chickens. "Please sit quietly and do not move," Marcella told Raggedy Ann. "If you move, you might fall and get hurt!"

So, Raggedy Ann sat quietly, just like Marcella told her. She smiled. She knew that she had fallen many times before and it had never hurt her. It was because she was filled with nice soft cotton!

玛塞拉跑回屋子去了。她将布娃娃安留在了栅栏上。栅栏附近有一群鸡。"请你安静地坐着，不要动，"玛塞拉吩咐布娃娃安说，"假如你乱动的话，说不定会掉下去摔伤的！"

于是，布娃娃安遵照玛塞拉的命令，一动不动地坐在那里，咧着大嘴巴在微笑。其实，她心里很清楚，自己曾经摔下过很多次，但是从来也没有受伤。因为她身体里填充的是柔软的新棉花！

Raggedy Ann Stories
布娃娃 安

Raggedy Ann sat there for a while. Then a little bird came. It flew to the flowers nearby. It came very close to Raggedy Ann's head.

Raggedy Ann turned her head to see the bird and lost her balance. Plump! She fell down among the chickens.

The chickens ran away in all directions, but a rooster named Old Ironsides stayed.

He was not happy. He put his head down close to the ground and made a strange noise as he looked angrily at Raggedy Ann.

Raggedy Ann only smiled at Old Ironsides, the rooster. She touched her hair with her hand and did not look at him. She was not afraid of him.

Then something strange happened. The old rooster jumped up in the air and kicked out his feet. He knocked Raggedy Ann over and over.

布娃娃安坐了一会儿，一只小鸟飞了过来。鸟儿飞到旁边的花丛里，离布娃娃的脑袋简直近在咫尺。

布娃娃安扭头去看小鸟，不小心失去了平衡。"砰"的一声，她掉进了鸡群里。

那群鸡吓得四散而逃，只有一只名叫铁甲军的大公鸡待在原地未动。

大公鸡很不高兴。它愤怒地瞪着布娃娃安，一边将脑袋贴近地面，发出一种奇怪的声音。

布娃娃安朝大公鸡铁甲军微微一笑。接着，她用手摸了一下头发，就不再理睬它了。她并不害怕大公鸡。

然而，奇怪的事情发生了。老公鸡腾空跳了起来，用两只爪子乱踢乱抓，害得布娃娃安一连翻了好几个跟斗。

Raggedy Ann shouted, "Shoo!" at the rooster to make him go away. Old Ironsides didn't run away. He kicked her again.

Two old hens had been watching the rooster kick Raggedy. Now, they ran to help her. One old hen stood in front of the rooster. The other old hen held Raggedy's dress and pulled her into the chicken coop.

It was dark inside. Raggedy felt the two friendly chickens pull her up over the nests.

Finally, when the old hens stopped pulling her, Raggedy could sit up. Her button eyes were very good, so she could see the old hen in front of her.

"Wow, that's the hardest work I've done in a long time!" said the old hen. "I was afraid Mr. Rooster would tear your dress!"

布娃娃安朝大公鸡发出"嘘"声，想把它赶走。可是老铁甲军非但没走，反而狠狠地踢了她一脚。

两只老母鸡站在一旁，观望大公鸡发威。这时，它们都跑上前来救助布娃娃。一只老母鸡挡在前面，另一只老母鸡叼着布娃娃安的裙子，把她拖到了鸡棚里边。

鸡棚里很暗。布娃娃可以感觉到，那两只友好的老母鸡拖着她经过了一些鸡窝。

最后，老母鸡们放开布娃娃安，她翻身坐了起来。她的纽扣眼睛视力极佳，能够看见面前的老母鸡。

"哎唷，这是很久以来我所做过的最最吃力的活儿！"老母鸡说，"我担心公鸡先生会撕破你的裙子！"

"That was a strange game he was playing, Mrs. Hen," said Raggedy Ann.

The old hen laughed, "He wasn't playing a game, he was fighting you!"

"Fighting!" Raggedy Ann was surprised.

"Oh yes!" the old hen answered. "Old Ironsides, the rooster, thought you were going to hurt some of the young chickens. So, he was fighting you!"

"I am sorry that I fell inside, I wouldn't hurt anyone," Raggedy Ann said.

"If we tell you a secret, you must promise not to tell Marcella!" said the old hens.

"I promise! Cross my candy heart!" said Raggedy Ann.

Then the two old hens took Raggedy Ann to the farthest corner of the chicken coop. There, behind a box, they had built two nests. Each old hen had ten eggs in her nest.

"If the people in the house knew about the eggs, they would take them all!" said the hens. "And then we could not have our babies!"

Raggedy Ann felt the eggs. They were nice and warm. "Now we will have to sit on the eggs and warm them up again!"

"母鸡太太，大公鸡玩的是一种奇怪的游戏。"布娃娃安说。

老母鸡哈哈大笑，说道："它可不是在玩游戏，而是在跟你打架！"

"打架！"布娃娃安这一惊可非同小可。

"啊是的！"老母鸡回答，"老铁甲军，那只大公鸡，误以为你想要伤害小鸡。所以，它才跟你打架！"

"很抱歉我不慎跌进了鸡群里。但是我绝对不会伤害任何人！"布娃娃安解释道。

"如果我们告诉你一个秘密，你必须起誓决不告诉玛塞拉！"老母鸡说。

"我保证！我对天起誓！"布娃娃安说。

于是，两只老母鸡将布娃娃安带到鸡棚深处的一个角落。原来，它们在一个盒子后面搭了两个鸡窝，每个窝里放了十枚鸡蛋。

"要是让房子里的人知道了，他们会把鸡蛋全部拿走的，"母鸡们说，"那样，我们就再也无法得到鸡宝宝了！"

布娃娃安摸了摸鸡蛋，鸡蛋的表面非常光滑温暖。"现在，我们必须卧在鸡蛋上，再次把它们捂热！"

The two old hens opened their wings and sat down on the nests.

"But how can the eggs grow if you sit on them?" asked Raggedy. "If Fido sits on any plants in the garden, the plants will not grow, Marcella says!"

"Eggs are different!" one of the old hens explained. "In order to make the eggs hatch, we must sit on them for three weeks so they don't get cold!"

"And at the end of the three weeks do the eggs grow into a plant?" asked Raggedy Ann.

"You must be thinking of eggplant!" cried one old hen. "These are chicken eggs. They don't grow into a plant. After they hatch, we will have a lovely family of soft, cute little chicks. We can hold them under our wings and love them dearly!"

"Have you been sitting on the eggs very long?" Raggedy asked.

"We don't know!" said one hen. "You see, we leave the nests only once in a while to eat and drink."

"We were going out to get a drink when you fell in the pen!" said one of the old hens.

说着，两只老母鸡伸展开翅膀，伏在了鸡蛋上。

"你们卧在鸡蛋上面，它们怎么能够生长呢？"布娃娃安说，"玛塞拉说过，如果菲逗卧在了花园里的植物上，植物便无法生长！"

"鸡蛋跟植物不一样，"一只老母鸡解释道，"为了让鸡蛋孵化出小鸡，我们必须在鸡蛋上伏卧三个星期，让它们一直保持恒温状态。"

"那么，三个星期以后，鸡蛋能够长成一株植物吗？"布娃娃安又问道。

"你的小脑袋瓜里想的一定是茄子（eggplant）！"老母鸡叫道，"这是鸡蛋，绝对不会变成植物的。等到鸡蛋孵化了，我们就能够拥有一群毛茸茸、可爱的小鸡娃啦！我们可以用翅膀来保护它们，尽心尽意地爱它们！"

"你们在鸡蛋上已经伏卧很久了吗？"布娃娃安问道。

"我们也不太清楚，"母鸡回答说，"你瞧，我们只是偶尔离开一下，去吃点东西喝点儿水。"

"你掉进鸡群里的时候，我们正打算去喝水。"另一只老母鸡说。

"I'm happy to sit on the eggs to keep them warm while you get something to eat and drink!" said Raggedy.

So the two old hens walked out of the coop to finish their meal. While they were gone, Raggedy Ann sat quietly on the warm eggs.

Suddenly, underneath her she heard something, "Pick, pick!"

Then she felt something move. "I hope it isn't a mouse!" Raggedy Ann said to herself. "I wish the old hens would come back."

When they came back and saw Raggedy Ann's face, they said, "What is it?"

Raggedy Ann stood up on her feet. She looked down. There were several little baby chicks, round and fluffy.

"Cheep! Cheep! Cheep!" they cried when Raggedy stepped out of the nest.

"Baby chicks!" Raggedy cried. She picked up one of the little fluffy balls up. "They want to be held!"

The two old hens' eyes were bright with happiness. They got on the nests and opened their soft warm wings. "The other eggs will hatch soon!" they said.

　　"那么你们去吃东西喝水吧，我非常乐意坐在鸡蛋上，帮助它们保持温度。"布娃娃说。

　　于是，两只老母鸡走出鸡窝，继续去吃它们的饭。布娃娃安则代替老母鸡，静静地坐在那些暖乎乎的鸡蛋上。

　　突然，她听到自己身子底下传来"笃笃"的声音。

　　随后，她感到有什么东西在动。"但愿那不是老鼠！"布娃娃安自言自语道，"我希望老母鸡们赶紧回来。"

　　老母鸡们回来了。看见布娃娃安焦虑的脸色，它们连忙问道："你怎么啦？"

　　布娃娃安迅速地站起身来，朝下面望去。啊，她看到了几只毛茸茸、圆滚滚的小鸡娃！

　　布娃娃安连忙从鸡蛋上下来。那几只小鸡娃"叽叽！叽叽！叽叽！"地叫着。

　　"鸡宝宝！"布娃娃嚷着，捧起一只毛茸茸的小圆球，"它们想让人用手托着自己！"

　　两只老母鸡喜形于色，立刻伏到了鸡蛋上，伸展开温暖的翅膀。"别的鸡蛋很快也要孵出小鸡来啦！"它们说。

So, for several days, Raggedy helped the two hens hatch the rest of the chicks. Just as they finished, Marcella came inside and looked around.

"How did you get in here, Raggedy Ann?" she cried. "I have been looking everywhere for you! Did the chickens pull you in here?"

Behind the box, both old hens talked softly to the chicks under their wings. Marcella heard them.

She lifted the box away and gave a little cry of surprise and happiness.

"Oh, dear old Hennypennies!" she cried, lifting both old hens from their nests. "You have hidden your nests! Now you have one, two, three, four—twenty chicks!" As she counted them, Marcella put them in her apron. Then she lifted Raggedy up and placed her over the new little chicks.

"Come on, Hennypennies!" she said, and went out of the coop. The two old hens followed right behind her.

Marcella called Daddy and told him about the new chicks. Daddy made two nice houses for the hens and their babies.

就这样，一连好几天，布娃娃都在帮助母鸡们孵育剩下的鸡蛋。没过多久，所有的小鸡都出壳了。就在这时，玛塞拉走进了鸡棚，四下里张望。

"布娃娃安，你怎么跑到这里面来啦？"她大声嚷道，"我满世界到处找你！是那些鸡把你拖进来的吗？"

在盒子后面，两只老母鸡把小鸡娃遮挡在翅膀底下，轻轻地安抚着它们。玛塞拉听到了它们的声音。

她把盒子挪开，顿时发出了惊喜的感叹。

"啊，亲爱的小母鸡潘妮！"她喊着，伸手将两只老母鸡提溜了起来，"你们竟然藏了一窝小鸡！你们竟然拥有，一、二、三、四——二十只小鸡！"她一边数着，一边将小鸡放在她的围裙里。最后，她一把抓起布娃娃，把她搁在了刚出生的鸡宝宝上面。

"来吧，小母鸡潘妮！"她说着，迈步走出了鸡棚。两只老母鸡乖乖地跟在她的身后。

玛塞拉叫来了爸爸，将小鸡宝宝的事情告诉了他。爸爸给鸡妈妈和鸡宝宝盖了两个漂亮的鸡窝。

All the dolls were happy when they heard of Raggedy's adventure. They did not have to wait long before Marcella took them out to see the new chicks.

听完布娃娃安的历险故事，娃娃们都高兴地松了一口气。没过多久，玛塞拉就带着他们，前去看望了鸡宝宝们。

After Reading

1. What happened when Raggedy Ann fell into the chicken coop?

2. What was the hens' secret?

3. Do you think Raggedy Ann was right to tell the hens' secret? When is it important to keep a secret and when is it important not to keep a secret?

Word List

 balance: *v.* to keep your body in control so you don't fall over

 rooster: *n.* a male chicken

 hen: *n.* a female chicken that lays eggs

 chicken coop: *n.* a small house on a farm where chickens can build their nests

 promise: *v.* to tell someone you will definitely do something or that something will definitely happen

cross my candy heart: *idiom.* "cross my heart" is an expression that children use when someone asks them to make a promise. It means, "Yes, I promise!" Raggedy Ann had a candy heart so she said "cross my candy heart."

 hatch: *v.* when baby chickens grow enough to come out of the egg, the egg breaks and the chicken leaves the egg

 eggplant: *n.* a kind of vegetable that has purple or white fruit; an eggplant is either long or round

 chick: *n.* a baby chicken

 fluffy: *adj.* soft and light (Example: The cat has fluffy hair.)

 apron: *n.* a piece of cloth used to protect your clothes when cooking or cleaning

12

Raggedy Ann and the Mouse

布娃娃安和小老鼠

Before Reading

1. Do you ever find small animals in your house? What do you do with them?

2. Look at the second picture. What is Uncle Clem pointing at?

3. What do you think happens in this story?

Every day Raggedy Ann woke up happy. But today Raggedy Ann was very angry. She had a frown on her face.

Someone or something had been in the dolls' room and left a trail of crumbs.

"It's such a mess!" said Raggedy Ann.

"Something must be done about it!" said Lisa. She was also very angry.

每天清晨，布娃娃安都会高高兴兴地醒来。可是今天，她却是满脸怒气，紧紧地皱着眉头。

原来，不知是谁来过娃娃们的房间，在地上留下了长长的一道碎屑。

"瞧瞧这个脏乱劲儿！"布娃娃安说。

"一定要采取行动，加以制止！"丽莎附和道。她同样感到非常气愤。

"When I catch who did this, I don't know what I will do with him!" said the Tin Soldier. He felt angry, too.

"It was a mouse! Here is the hole he came from," said Uncle Clem. "Come, see!"

All the dolls ran to Uncle Clem. He was down on his hands and knees.

"This must be the place," said Raggedy Ann. "We will cover the hole. He will not come out again!"

The dolls found old clothes and pieces of paper. They pushed them into the mouse's hole.

"I thought I heard a mouse last night," one of the penny dolls said.

Marcella came to the dolls' room. When Marcella saw the crumbs, she ran downstairs. She told Daddy and Mamma about it. They came upstairs with her. Soon, they also found the mouse's hole.

Later that day, Marcella came running into their room. She had a small kitten in her arms.

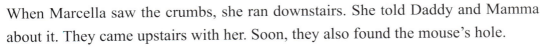

"等抓住了干坏事儿的那个小子，看我怎么收拾他！"白铁士兵说，他也很生气。

"是老鼠干的！这儿有一个老鼠出入的洞口。"克莱姆叔叔说，"快来看哪！"所有的娃娃都朝克莱姆叔叔跑了过去，他正匍匐在一个洞口前面。

"肯定是这个地方，"布娃娃安说，"我们把洞口堵上，它就再也进不来了！"娃娃们找来了纸张和旧衣服，用它们堵住了老鼠洞。

"我想，昨夜我听到了老鼠的声音。"一个瓷娃娃说。

这时，玛塞拉走进了玩具室。看见那些碎屑，她马上跑下楼去了。她把这件事告诉了爸爸和妈妈。他们跟着她一起来到楼上。片刻之间，他们便发现了老鼠洞。

那天后晌，玛塞拉怀里抱着一只小猫，跑进了房间。

Marcella showed the kitten to all the dolls.

"Her name is Boots," said Marcella. "See, she has four little white feet!"

Boots was a happy kitten. She played with the penny dolls. She jumped at them from behind the chairs. All of them had a lot of fun.

Soon, Marcella left the room. Then Raggedy Ann played with Boots. They rolled around on the floor. They liked each other and enjoyed themselves.

Boots slept on top of Raggedy Ann. The kitten was heavy but Raggedy Ann was very glad to have Boots sleep with her.

At night, Boots started to cry for her Mommy. She missed her Momma. It was the first time she had been away from home. Raggedy Ann talked to her and made her feel better. Soon, Boots went back to sleep.

Within a few days, Boots had become friends with all the dolls. She did not cry at night. The dolls told her about the mouse. She said that she would look for him at night.

One night, all the dolls were sleeping. Only Boots was awake. Then a small mouse came out of the hole. Boots jumped after the mouse. She hit the toy piano. The piano made a lot of noise and the dolls woke up.

玛塞拉向娃娃们介绍了小猫。

"它的名字叫皮靴，"玛塞拉说，"瞧，它长着四只雪白的小爪子！"

皮靴是只快活的小猫。它跟瓷娃娃们一道儿玩耍，从椅子背后跳到他们身上。大家玩得不亦乐乎。

过了一会儿，玛塞拉出去了。布娃娃安也跟皮靴嬉戏起来。他们俩在地板上打滚，彼此都很喜欢对方，玩得甭提多爽了！

皮靴喜欢躺在布娃娃安的身上睡觉。小猫咪很重，可是，布娃娃安乐于跟皮靴挤在一起。

那天夜里，皮靴开始哭着喊妈妈。它思念自己的妈妈。因为这是它头一次离开家。布娃娃安竭力安慰小猫咪，使它慢慢地安静了下来。很快，皮靴又睡着了。

没过几天，皮靴跟所有的娃娃都成了好朋友。夜里它不再哭叫了。娃娃们向它讲述了老鼠曾经来捣乱的事情。皮靴说，自己半夜要爬起来逮老鼠。

一天夜里，娃娃们睡得正香，皮靴独自在守候着。突然，一只小老鼠从洞里跑了出来。皮靴马上朝老鼠扑了过去。但是，它不小心碰到了玩具钢琴。钢琴发出了巨大的声响，将娃娃们全都惊醒了。

They ran over to Boots. She was sitting with a little mouse in her mouth.

The mouse was squeaking loudly!

Raggedy Ann did not like to hear it squeak. But she did not want the mouse to leave a mess again either.

So, Raggedy Ann said to the tiny little mouse, "You should not come here. Why don't you go out to live in the barn?"

"I am not hurting anyone!" squeaked the little mouse. "This is the first time I have ever been here!"

"Aren't you the little mouse who left all the crumbs?" Raggedy Ann asked.

"No," the little mouse answered. "I was visiting the mice inside the walls. I live in the barn and have three baby mice. I did not leave any crumbs."

"Are you a Mamma mouse?" Uncle Clem asked.

"Yes!" the little mouse squeaked. "If the kitten will let me go, I will run home to my children. I will never come back here."

"Let her go, Boots!" the dolls said. "She has three little baby mice at home! Please let her go!"

他们爬起身来，朝着皮靴跑了过去。只见皮靴坐在地上，嘴里衔着一只小老鼠。那只老鼠正在吱吱地大声尖叫。

布娃娃安不忍心听到老鼠的叫声，可是，她也不愿意让老鼠把房间搞得乱七八糟。

布娃娃安对小老鼠说："你不应该到这里来。你为什么不待在外面的库房里呢？"

"我从来没有伤害过任何人！"小老鼠吱吱叫道，"我是第一次来这个地方！"

"难道上次弄得满地都是碎屑的老鼠不是你吗？"布娃娃安问道。

"不是我，"小老鼠答道，"我是来墙里边的老鼠家做客的。我住在库房里，我还有三只老鼠宝宝。我从来没有留下过什么碎屑。"

"你是个老鼠妈妈？"克莱姆叔叔问道。

"是的！"小老鼠吱吱叫着，"如果小猫放了我，我马上就跑回家去，回到老鼠宝宝们的身边。我再也不来这里啦。"

"皮靴，放它走吧！"娃娃们求情道，"它家里还有三只老鼠宝宝！求你放了它吧！"

"No," Boots told them. "This is the first mouse I have ever caught. I want to eat her!" The little Mamma mouse began squeaking even more loudly.

"If you do not let the Mamma mouse go, Boots, I will be very sad, and I will not want to play with you," said Raggedy Ann.

"Raggedy will not play with Boots," said all of the dolls. All of them liked to play with Raggedy Ann. They would be very sad if she did not play with them. So they thought Boots would feel sad too.

But Boots did not let the little Mamma mouse go.

The dolls talked together. While they talked, Boots played with the mouse. She let the little mouse go, and then when the mouse ran, she caught it again.

She did this again and again until the poor mouse grew very tired and could not run.

Raggedy Ann watched the little mouse try to run away. But Boots caught it every time. This made Raggedy Ann very sad. Tears came to her eyes.

Boots started to jump after the little mouse again. This time Raggedy Ann threw her arms around the kitten's neck. "Run, Mamma mouse!" Raggedy Ann shouted as she held the kitten. The mouse was too tired to run.

"不行，"皮靴回答说，"这是我逮住的第一只老鼠。我想要吃了它！"听到这话，小老鼠妈妈更加大声地尖叫起来。

"皮靴，如果你不放走老鼠妈妈，我会感到非常伤心的。我再也不跟你一块儿玩啦。"布娃娃安说。

"布娃娃安再也不跟皮靴玩啦！"所有的娃娃们重复道。他们都爱跟布娃娃安玩耍。如果她不跟他们玩儿，他们一定会感到难过的。所以，娃娃们以为，皮靴也会因此而感到难过。

可是，皮靴就是不肯放走小老鼠妈妈。

娃娃们围聚在一起议论纷纷。这工夫，皮靴开始戏弄小老鼠。它松开爪子，老鼠刚一跑开，它就一把又抓住了它。

小猫一遍又一遍地捉弄老鼠，到后来，可怜的小老鼠精疲力竭，再也跑不动了。

布娃娃安眼睁睁地看着，小老鼠一次次地试图逃命，可是，每一次都被皮靴重新抓了回来。这个场景令布娃娃安感到十分心痛，她的眼睛里噙满了泪水。

皮靴又一次放开小老鼠，正准备扑上前去。不料布娃娃安突然伸出双臂，搂住了小猫的脖子。"老鼠妈妈，快跑！"布娃娃安搂着小猫，大声喊道。可是，小老鼠已经累得跑不动了。

Uncle Clem ran and pushed the Mamma mouse into the hole. Then the little mouse was gone.

When Raggedy Ann took her arms from around Boots, the kitten was very angry. She scratched Raggedy Ann with her claws.

But Raggedy Ann only smiled. It did not hurt her at all. Boots felt ashamed. She went over and lay down near the hole in the wall. She waited for the mouse to come back. But the mouse never returned. She was with her baby mice in the barn.

Raggedy Ann and the dolls went to bed. In the night, Raggedy Ann felt something jump up on her bed. It was Boots. Boots licked Raggedy's face. Raggedy Ann smiled happily to herself. Once again Boots slept on top of Raggedy Ann.

Raggedy Ann knew that Boots was not angry with her for helping Mamma Mouse.

克莱姆叔叔跑上前去，一把将老鼠妈妈推进了洞里。就这样，小老鼠逃走了。

布娃娃安这才松开双臂。小猫咪气坏了，它用爪子狠狠地抓挠布娃娃安。

可是，布娃娃安依旧笑容可掬。小猫的抓挠并没有使她感到疼痛。皮靴感到很是羞愧。转身走开了。它在老鼠洞的旁边躺卧下来，期待着小老鼠还会重新出来。然而，那只老鼠再也不敢来了。此刻，它正在库房与自己的鼠宝宝们待在一起。

布娃娃安和娃娃们返回到床上继续睡觉。夜里，布娃娃安感到有个什么东西跳到了她的床上。原来那是皮靴。皮靴舔了一下布娃娃的脸。布娃娃安高兴地咧着嘴笑了起来。皮靴又躺到了布娃娃安的身上。

布娃娃安心里明白，尽管自己放走了老鼠妈妈，皮靴还是原谅了她。

After Reading

1. Why did the mouse come in the house and how did it leave?

2. What did Raggedy Ann do to save the mouse?

3. Raggedy Ann and Boots did not agree about what to do with the mouse. What can happen when people disagree?

Word List

frown: *n.*　the opposite of a smile; a sad face

crumb: *n.*　a very small piece of dry food, usually bread

squeak: *v.*　to make a loud, high noise

claw: *n.*　a cat's or bird's sharp fingernail

13

Raggedy Ann's New Sisters
布娃娃安的新姐妹

Before Reading

1. Imagine something you own is copied hundreds of times and given to children around the world. What would you want to have copied?

2. Look at the picture on page 103. Why do you think there are so many Raggedy Anns all together?

3. How many new sisters do you think Raggedy Ann will have? Where do you think they will come from?

Marcella was having a tea party up in her room when Daddy called her. She left the dolls around the little table and ran downstairs. She took Raggedy Ann with her.

Mamma, Daddy, and their friend John were talking in the living room. Marcella had never met John so Daddy introduced them to each other.

玛塞拉正在房间里举办茶点派对，突然听见爸爸在外面喊她。她把娃娃们留在了餐桌旁边，自己带着布娃娃安跑下楼去。

爸爸、妈妈和他们的朋友约翰坐在起居室里聊天。玛塞拉以前没有见过约翰，于是，爸爸介绍他们互相认识。

He was a big man with kind eyes and a nice smile. His smile was as pleasant as Raggedy Ann's. Because Daddy, Mamma and Marcella liked him, Raggedy Ann liked him too.

"I have two little girls," he told Marcella. "Their names are Virginia and Doris. Doris has a doll called Freddy. One time, we were at the beach. They were playing in the sand and they covered Freddy in the sand. After they covered Freddy, they went farther down the beach to play. They forgot all about Freddy.

"When it was time for us to go home, Virginia and Doris remembered Freddy. They ran back to get him, but the waves came and pulled Freddy out into the water. They saw Freddy go under the water and they could not find him again. Virginia and Doris were very sad and they talked about Freddy all the way home."

"It was too bad they forgot Freddy," said Marcella.

"Yes, it was!" John said as he took Raggedy Ann up and made her dance on Marcella's knee. "But it was okay after all, because, do you know what happened to Freddy?"

"No, what happened to him?" Marcella asked.

约翰是个身材高大的人，长着一双善良的眼睛，脸上带着和蔼的微笑。他的微笑跟布娃娃安的微笑一样令人感到愉快。由于爸爸、妈妈和玛塞拉都喜欢约翰，布娃娃安也对他颇有好感。

"我有两个小姑娘，"他告诉玛塞拉说，"她们的名字叫弗吉尼亚和多丽丝。多丽丝有一个名叫弗雷迪的娃娃。有一回，我们到海滨度假。孩子们在沙滩上面玩耍，将弗雷迪埋到了沙土里。接着，她们跑到远处的海滩去玩儿，把弗雷迪忘到了九霄云外。

"到了该回家的时候，弗吉尼亚和多丽丝这才想起弗雷迪。她们急忙跑回去找他。不料，海浪已经将弗雷迪冲走了。她们眼睁睁地看着弗雷迪沉到水里，再也看不见了。弗吉尼亚和多丽丝难过极了，在回家的路上，她们不停地谈论着弗雷迪。"

"她们把弗雷迪给忘了，这实在太糟糕了！"玛塞拉说。

"是的，一点不错！"约翰说着，拿起了布娃娃安。他拉着她的手在玛塞拉的腿上跳起舞来。"不过，最后的结局却是皆大欢喜，噢，你知道弗雷迪的遭遇吗？"

"不知道，他怎么啦？"玛塞拉急忙问道。

"Well, first of all, when Freddy was covered with the sand, he enjoyed it very much. He didn't mind when the waves came up over him. He thought Virginia and Doris would come back and get him.

"But then Freddy felt the sand above him move. It felt as if someone was getting him out. Soon his head was uncovered. Now he could look right up through the beautiful green water. What do you think was happening?

"The waves were washing away the sand and uncovering Freddy. When he was completely uncovered, the undertow pulled him out to sea. Then the waves threw him up into the air with the ocean spray. The wind and the waves helped carry him back to the beach."

Marcella couldn't wait to hear what happened next.

"The next day, Virginia and Doris found him on the beach, looking very happy after his wonderful adventure!"

"Freddy must have enjoyed it and your little girls must be very glad to have Freddy back again!" said Marcella. "Raggedy Ann went up in the air on the tail of a kite one day and fell and was lost. So now I am very careful with her!"

　　"嗯，起初，当弗雷迪被埋在沙土中的时候，他感到非常愉快。海浪扑打到他的身上，他一点儿也不在乎。他相信，弗吉尼亚和多丽丝一定会来找他的。

　　"但就在这时，弗雷迪感到自己身上的沙土在移动，仿佛有人正在把他从沙土中拖出来。很快，他的脑袋露了出来。透过清澈碧绿的海水，他可以看到外面的一切。你们猜猜看，到底发生了什么事情？

　　"原来，大浪将弗雷迪身上的沙子完全冲刷掉了，将他暴露了出来。这时，离岸的海浪裹挟着他奔涌到了海里。然后，波浪将他和浪花一起抛在了空中，风浪又把他冲回到了海滩上。"

　　玛塞拉迫不及待地想知道后来所发生的事情。

　　"第二天，弗吉尼亚和多丽丝在海滩上发现了弗雷迪。他经历了一场惊心动魄的历险，看上去显得特别开心！"

　　"弗雷迪肯定很享受那种经历。你的小姑娘重新得到弗雷迪，想必也非常高兴！"玛塞拉说，"有一天，我们把布娃娃安绑在风筝的尾巴上，让她飞上了天空，结果她却摔了下来，差点儿找不到了。从那以后，我对她总是格外小心！"

"Would you let me take Raggedy Ann for a few days?" asked John.

Marcella was quiet. She liked the man, but she did not want to lose Raggedy Ann.

"I promise to take very good care of her and I'll give her back to you in a week. Will you let her go with me, Marcella?"

Marcella finally agreed and when John left, he put Raggedy Ann in his bag.

"It is lonely without Raggedy Ann!" said the dolls each night.

"We miss her happy, painted smile and her fun ways!" they said.

And so the week went by slowly....

When Raggedy Ann finally came back, all the dolls wanted to hug Raggedy Ann and ask her many questions. They could hardly wait until the time when Marcella left them alone.

They hugged Raggedy Ann almost out of shape! She had to straighten her hair and feel her button eyes to see if they were still there. Then she said, "Well, what have you been doing? Tell me all the news!"

　　"你愿意让我把布娃娃安带回家几天吗？"约翰问道。

玛塞拉沉默了。她喜欢约翰，可是，她又不舍得与布娃娃安分开。

　　"我保证尽力照顾好她。一个星期以后，我一定把她归还给你。玛塞拉，你同意把布娃娃安借给我吗？"

考虑再三，玛塞拉最后还是同意了。临走之前，约翰把布娃娃安放进了他的提包。

那几天，一到晚上，娃娃们就会感叹道："布娃娃安不在家，实在是太寂寞了！"

　　"我们想念她无忧无虑的笑容，还有她那有趣的言谈举止！"他们说。

一个星期的时光缓缓地流逝过去了。

布娃娃安终于回家了。所有的娃娃都期盼着能够上前去拥抱她，并且问她许许多多的问题。他们急不可耐地等着玛塞拉离开，因为只有到那个时候他们才能自由行动。

　　玛塞拉离开后，娃娃们一拥而上，使劲儿地拥抱布娃娃安，使她差点儿脱了形！布娃娃安整理了一下自己的头发，摸了摸纽扣眼睛，看它们是否安然无恙。这时，她才开口说道，"好啦，这些天你们都做了些什么事儿呀？快把所有的新闻都告诉我！"

"Oh we just had the usual tea parties and games!" said the Tin Soldier. "Tell us about yourself, Raggedy, we missed you so much!"

"Yes! Tell us where you have been and what you have done, Raggedy!" all the dolls said.

Just then, Raggedy Ann saw that one of the penny dolls was missing a hand.

"How did this happen?" she asked as she picked up the doll.

"I fell off the table and hit the Tin Soldier last night when we were playing. But don't worry about a little thing like that, Raggedy Ann," the penny doll said. "Tell us about yourself! Did you have a nice time?"

"I will not say anything until your hand is fixed!" Raggedy Ann said.

So Helen ran and found a bottle of glue. "Where's the hand?" Raggedy asked.

"In my pocket," the penny doll answered.

Raggedy Ann glued the penny doll's hand in place and put a piece of cloth around it to hold it until the glue dried. Then she said, "When I tell you about this wonderful adventure, I know you will all feel very happy. It made me almost burst with joy."

　　"哦，我们刚刚参加了茶点聚会，还做了一些游戏！"白铁士兵开腔说道，"布娃娃安，给我们讲讲你的故事吧，我们都非常想念你！"

　　"对！布娃娃安，给我们讲讲你去了什么地方，做了些什么事情。"全体娃娃同声响应道。

　　就在这个当口，布娃娃安发现一个瓷娃娃少了一只手。

　　"这是怎么搞的？"她抱起那个瓷娃娃，问道。

　　"昨天晚上，我们做游戏的时候，我不小心从桌子上摔了下去，掉在了白铁士兵的身上。布娃娃安，别操心这微不足道的小事了，"瓷娃娃说，"给我们讲讲你自己的经历吧！这些天你过得愉快吗？"

　　"在你的手修复好之前，我绝对不会讲任何事情！"布娃娃安说。

　　于是，海伦跑去拿来了一瓶胶水。"那只手在哪儿？"布娃娃安问道。

　　"在我的口袋里，"瓷娃娃回答。

　　布娃娃安将瓷娃娃的手接好，然后用一块布包扎起来，等待胶水将伤口固定。这时，她才开口说道："我来给你们讲讲我的奇妙经历吧。我知道，大家听了都会非常开心的。因为这个经历确实让我满心欢喜。"

Raggedy Ann Stories
布娃娃 安

The dolls all sat on the floor around Raggedy Ann. The Tin Soldier sat with his arm over her shoulder.

"Well, first, when I left," said Raggedy Ann, "I was put in John's bag. It was stuffy in there, but I did not mind it. I think I fell asleep. When I woke up, I saw John's hand. Then the hand took me out from the bag. John danced me on his knee. 'What do you think of her?' he asked three other people sitting nearby.

"I was so interested in looking out of the window that I did not listen to what they said. We were on a train and the scenery was just flying by! Then I was put back in the bag.

"The next time I was taken from the bag, I was in a large, clean, bright room and there were many, many workers all dressed in white aprons.

"John showed me to the people in aprons. Then they cut my seams and took out my cotton. And what do you think? They found my lovely candy heart! It had not melted at all as I thought. They put me on a clean white cloth on a table. Then they drew all around my body with a pencil. After that, they filled me with cotton again and dressed me.

娃娃们围坐在布娃娃安四周的地板上，白铁士兵伸出一只手臂搂住她的肩膀。

"好吧，当我离开家的时候，"布娃娃安说，"约翰把我放进了他的提包里。提包里面很是憋闷，可是我并不在乎。我想自己是睡着了。等我醒来，我看见了约翰的手。接着，他把我从提包里取了出来，让我在他的腿上跳舞。'你们觉得她怎么样？'他向坐在附近的另外三个人问道。

"我兴致勃勃地望着窗外，没有留心听他们讲了些什么。我们正坐在一辆火车里，窗外的风景全都一闪而过！后来，约翰又把我放进了提包。

"当他再次把我从提包里取出来的时候，我已经来到一间宽敞、洁净而明亮的房间，周围有许多穿着白色围裙的工人。

"约翰把我展示给那些穿白色围裙的人们。随后，他们拆开我的接缝，掏出里面的棉花。你们猜怎么着？他们发现了我那颗可爱的心形糖果！出乎我的预料，那颗糖一点儿都没有融化。他们把我放在桌面一块干净的白布上。接着，他们用铅笔环绕着我的身体描画了一圈。然后，他们把棉花重新填充回去，帮我穿戴整齐。

"I stayed in that clean, big, and bright room for two or three days and nights. I watched my sisters grow from pieces of cloth into dolls just like myself!"

"Your SISTERS!" the dolls all shouted in astonishment. "What do you mean, Raggedy?"

"I mean," said Raggedy Ann, "that John borrowed me from Marcella so that he could make dolls exactly like me. Before I left the big clean room, there were hundreds of dolls. They are so much like me you wouldn't be able to say which one is me and which one is not."

"We could tell it's you by your happy smile!" said Lisa.

"But all of my sister dolls have smiles just like mine!" answered Raggedy Ann.

　　"我在那个洁净、高大而明亮的车间里待了两三个昼夜。我亲眼目睹了我的姐妹们由布片变成布娃娃的整个过程！"

　　"你的姐妹们！"娃娃们惊呼道，"布娃娃，你这话是什么意思呀？"

　　"我的意思是，"布娃娃安答道，"约翰把我从玛塞拉那里借来，为的是要制作跟我一模一样的布娃娃。等到我离开那个宽敞整洁的车间时，他们已经制作出了好几百个布娃娃。她们都跟我长得非常相像，人们很难将我与她们分辨出来。"

　　"凭借你快乐的微笑，我们可以将你辨认出来！"丽莎说。

　　"可是，我那些布娃娃姐妹们都有着同样的微笑！"布娃娃安回答。

"And button eyes?" the dolls all asked.

"Yes, button eyes!" Raggedy Ann said.

"I would know that it's you because of your dress, Raggedy Ann," said Lisa. "Your dress is fifty years old!"

"But my new sister rag dolls have dresses just like mine. John used cloth for their dresses that was exactly like the cloth in my dress."

"I know how we could tell you from the other dolls, even if you all look exactly alike!" Helen said. She had been thinking for a long time.

"How?" asked Raggedy Ann with a laugh.

"By feeling your candy heart! If the doll has a candy heart then it is you, Raggedy Ann!"

Raggedy Ann laughed, "I'm so glad you all love me so much, but I am sure you wouldn't be able to tell me from my new sisters, except that I'm old and worn. Each new doll has a candy heart, too! On each heart are the words 'I LOVE YOU' just like my own candy heart."

"她们都有纽扣眼睛吗？"娃娃们齐声问道。

"是的，都有纽扣眼睛！"布娃娃安答道。

"布娃娃安，凭着你的裙子，我便能认出你来，"丽莎说，"你的裙子已经有五十年的历史了！"

"但是，我的布娃娃新姐妹们穿着同样的裙子。约翰给她们做裙子用的布料跟我的不差分毫。"

"我知道如何将你跟别的布娃娃区分出来，即便你们长得一模一样！"海伦说。她已经默默地思考了很长时间。

"如何区分呢？"布娃娃安笑着问她。

"摸一摸你的糖果心脏！布娃娃安，那个有糖果心脏的布娃娃一定是你！"

布娃娃安哈哈大笑起来，"我很高兴，你们大家这么爱我。不过，我坚信，你们全都无法将我与我的新姐妹们分辨出来，因为每个新娃娃都有一颗糖果心脏！而且跟我的糖果心脏一样，上面写着'我爱你们'。我猜，唯一的区别是我已经有点破旧。"

"And there are hundreds and hundreds of the new dolls like you?" asked the little penny dolls.

"Hundreds and hundreds of them, all named Raggedy Ann," said Raggedy.

"Then," said the penny dolls, "we are really happy and proud of you! The new Raggedy Ann dolls will bring the love and happiness that you give to others."

"那就是说，有数以百计的、跟你一模一样的新布娃娃？"瓷娃娃们问道。

"是的，有成百上千的新娃娃，她们的名字都叫布娃娃安。"布娃娃回答。

"那样的话，"瓷娃娃们说，"我们真的为你感到骄傲，为你感到快乐！那些新布娃娃安将会像你一样，把爱和幸福带给其他的人们。"

After Reading

1. How did Raggedy Ann get new sisters?

2. In what ways was Raggedy Ann the same as her sisters? How was she different?

3. Raggedy Ann's friends were at first afraid that they wouldn't be able to tell her from the other dolls, but in the end they were happy. Do you think special things should be copied? Why or why not?

Word List

introduce: *v.*   to tell someone who a new person is

beach: *n.*   the place right next to the water of an ocean or sea; there is usually sand on a beach

wave: *n.*   movement of water that moves up and down and back and forth

undertow: *n.*   the water under the sea that pulls away from the land

spray: *n.*   tiny drops of water that fly in the air

missing: *adj.*   gone, not there anymore

glue: *n.*   liquid that makes things stay together

burst with joy: *idiom.*   to be very happy and excited

stuffy: *adj.*   hard to breathe from being in a very small space

scenery: *n.*   nature all around that you can see

astonishment: *n.*   a big surprise